P.C. HAWKE mysteries

THE SURFING CORPSE

PAUL ZINDEL

Cat

Feb, 2003

VOLO

Hyperion
New York

Copyright © 2001 by Paul Zindel

Volo and the Volo colophon are trademarks of Disney Enterprises, Inc. All rights reserved. No part of this book may be reproduced or transmitted in any form or by any means, electronic or mechanical, including photocopying, recording, or by any information storage and retrieval system, without written permission from the publisher. For information address Volo Books, 114 Fifth Avenue, New York, New York 10011-5690.

First Edition
1 3 5 7 9 10 8 6 4 2

The text for this book is set in Janson Text 11.5/15.
Photo of thunderstorm: Don Farrall
Photo of man surfing: PhotoLink
Photo of Oneonta Falls: Russell Illig

Library of Congress Catalog Card Number on file.
ISBN 0-7868-1573-6
Visit www.volobooks.com

Contents

From the terrifying files of P.C. Hawke:

THE SURFING CORPSE • Case #2

Case #2 began something like this:

Have you ever heard the expression, "There's more to this than meets the eye?" Of course you have. It's an old cliché. But like most clichés, it's got some truth to it.

One time, this Russian guy Potemkin actually built a whole village of fake, prosperous-looking house fronts just to make visitors think things were peachy, when of course they weren't. But don't go thinking Potemkin was the only one. There are all kinds of "Potemkin villages" in life.

For instance, years ago the famous magician David Copperfield made the Statue of Liberty disappear—or did he? It's not too hard to fool the masses.

So what, you ask? Well, when you're a detective—like me, P.C. Hawke, and my friend and colleague, Mackenzie Riggs—separating illusion from reality is your mission. That's why the old cliché "There's more to this than meets the eye" keeps coming back to haunt us.

I mean, you think somebody is dead and buried. You mourn them, maybe you cry, and then you get on with your life.

And then, you see the dead man walking. I don't mean like that movie about death row. I mean for real. That's what happened to Mackenzie and me—we actually saw a dead man walking.

Or rather, surfing.

As always, recording the truth and nothing but the truth (although sometimes it's difficult to tell what the truth really is)—I am,

P.C. Hawke

(a.k.a. Peter Christopher Hawke)

Heaven Falls

It all started about six weeks ago, with a perfectly normal school trip on a perfectly normal fall day. Of course, when you're talking about our school—Westside School—nothing's ever *really* normal. Westside is an expensive, private academy, where the students are all either rich, famous, or on some kind of special freaky scholarship. We are probably the motliest collection of overprivileged, gifted, demented, neurotic teenagers in all of New York City—and when you consider that the city's population is about eight million, that's saying a lot.

The other kids at Westside will tell you that Mackenzie and I are the weird ones. "Wherever they go, people start getting killed left and right," is the buzz around school these days. And I have to admit, it's sort of true.

But trust me, it's not our fault. Can you blame us if a high-ranking scientist at the American Museum of Natural History got herself murdered? Was it our fault that we noticed that a mannequin in the window at

Bloomingdale's was really a nicely made-up *corpse*?

We just happen to be observant—okay, nosy—and well-connected. And yes, we like to see justice done. But does that make us weird, I ask you?

For instance, take Cubby Katz. *Please*. *Take* him. Get this—he's saving his fingernail and toenail clippings in a jar in his freezer, so they can clone him in case he should step in front of a truck.

Not weird enough for you? Try Kendra Morganstern. Her pet ferret finally died, after lying in a coma for three years. You'd think "enough already, go and bury poor Frisky (who isn't so frisky anymore) in the backyard." But no. Kendra had the thing stuffed, and hung it up in her bedroom with an altar in front of it. I guess you have to admire her devotion to her pet. But it's gross and creepy, if you ask me. Needless to say, Kendra doesn't get a lot of visitors.

And then, there's Timmy Warner. Or at least, there *was* Timmy, until the day of our Junior Class Retreat. It was the morning of September twenty-ninth that we headed west to the Delaware Water Gap National Recreation Area in a tour bus, with some chaperoning parents on board, and others bringing up the rear in their minivans and BMWs. Timmy was actually sitting next to Mackenzie on the bus, his big, musclebound body planted between her and the aisle.

Mackenzie kept giving me her eye-rolling, get-me-out-of-here look. Timmy was not her favorite personality at school—although lately she seemed to be *his* favorite.

You'd have thought a semi-good-looking guy like Timmy would have been able to get at least a trial date with Mackenzie. If you wrote a personals ad for him, it would read, "Brains and brawn—totally hot high school junior, quasi-successful commercial actor/model, National Honor Society member . . ." Which is why personals ads are so misleading. Timmy was all those things—but he was also superficial, self-absorbed, and coldhearted. In short, a total social barbarian.

At least Mackenzie could see right through the glare of Timmy's minor celebrity—not many of our female classmates could. My theory is that this is exactly why Timmy was giving Mac the full-court press: you always want what you can't have, right?

Anyway, the one thing I will give Timmy is that he was a hardworking minor actor (although his performance as Tarzan in that Snickers ad didn't do anything for me. Then again, I'm no Madison Avenue mogul—maybe Snickers fans loved it).

Timmy's mom had pushed him into acting, the same way she'd pushed his older sister, Marina (who had big blue eyes and a face like a pancake). Marina Warner used to go to Westside, too, until one day, she suddenly dropped out and disappeared.

Later, we heard she'd moved to California to act full-time. Every once in a while, you'd see her flapjack face in the background of some movie, but I understood she wasn't doing so hot out there in La-La Land.

Having a stage mother isn't usually a recipe for perfect mental health, and the Warners were no exception. Marina had definitely popped her fair share of Prozac, but there was no telling how wacked out Timmy really was. He kept it hidden better than his sister, though he did like to wear T-shirts with controversial slogans like JESUS WAS RAISED IN A KOSHER HOME.

As you may have guessed by now, I never personally liked the guy, and I wasn't the only one. He dated a lot of desperate girls, sure, but it never lasted long. He had hardly any close friends, either. *None*, in fact. And as we were about to find out, even his own mother couldn't stand him.

So now, here he was, bothering Mackenzie. I thought about telling him to knock it off, but I decided not to, remembering that the ride was almost over. Furthermore, I knew Mackenzie was a big girl and could take care of herself.

Boy, was she mad when we finally got off the bus! "Thanks a lot!" she snapped as we grabbed our backpacks, which were stuffed full of picnic lunches and sweatshirts. We headed up the path, following our fearless leader for the day, Ms. Conlan.

A sign at the side of the path read: HEAVEN FALLS PICNIC AREA, ½ MILE. The path led up a steep hillside. To the left, when there were gaps in the trees, we could see a spectacular waterfall. The Delaware River roared between two cliffs, then poured itself down a fifty-foot waterfall into a pool filled with sharp rocks.

Off to one side of the falls, a concrete spillway led down and around the rocks. At the far end, it disappeared into a building marked DELAWARE HYDROELECTRIC PLANT.

"I pity any poor fish caught up in that spillway," I commented. "The turbines inside that building would grind it up into fish food faster than you could say 'Chicken of the Sea.'"

Mackenzie didn't even look. "Stop trying to distract me, P.C.!" she snapped. "Why didn't you rescue me from that Neanderthal?"

"What am I, your white knight? Anyway, I didn't think it was my business."

"Well, what a drag to be trapped with Weenie Warner the whole way here," Mackenzie said with a sigh. "It's weird, though. Spend enough time with someone and you can always find something in common with them."

That's Mackenzie for you. Always analyzing things. It's what makes her such a great detective partner. She's got an instinctive feel for what makes people tick. I must say, though, that I failed to see what she and Timmy could possibly have in common besides the air they breathed.

"We both have issues with our parents and money," she went on. "My mom and dad are always complaining about how they don't have enough loot to do this or that," she said, kicking a pebble for emphasis. "Living in New York really sucks up the big bucks."

"What, did you ask for a raise in your allowance or something?" I asked.

"*Everybody* in school gets more than I do!" Mackenzie complained. Obviously, I'd nailed the problem. "You know me, P.C. I'm the maharina of the consignment shops, right? It's not like I go out and waste money."

"No," I agreed. "You do like to shop for bargains."

"Right!" She clucked her tongue, and added in a sarcastic voice, "But no, they have to save up to fix the roof."

Mackenzie and I like hanging out on her roof. Tar Beach, we call it. The Riggs family lives in this old brownstone on 70th Street, near Central Park West, and the roof is one of the coolest places I know. It's got a view out over the park that's just perfect for checking out the in-line skaters, Frisbee tossers, stroller pushers, drug sellers, and schizos screaming at the sky.

As I say, it's a great roof; but I have to admit, it could use some resurfacing.

"So, like, last week, there I was, *sewing the holes in my socks*," she went on.

"Darn."

"What, are you mocking me?"

"You were *darning*, not sewing," I corrected her. (Ah, yes, all those *New York Times* crossword puzzles sure do come in handy when you want to tick off your friends!)

"P.C., shut up, okay?" she said.

"Nice waterfall, huh?" I said, changing the subject.

Mackenzie looked at it for the first time. "Wow! That is fab and brill."

We had arrived at the top of the slope, where the picnic area beckoned, so I never got the chance to ask her more about Timmy's freakazoid problems. It didn't matter, though. I found out soon enough.

Up here, there were volleyball nets and a pathetic soccer field, and even some handy antique Port-o-potties near the picnic area.

"All right, everyone," Ms. Conlan announced, using her battery-powered bullhorn. "We eat in one hour. After that, I'm leading a hike to the top of the falls. For now, who wants to play volleyball?"

Mackenzie and I, ignoring Ms. Conlan's schedule, started digging right in to our lunches. We were already hungry, and we both wanted to chill out a little bit after the hike. Most of the other kids got involved in a nerdy volleyball game. Other student luminaries were sitting around gossiping or kicking back for a nap in the sun. A couple of girls were painting some mini-masterpieces on their fake nails. And three loser guys were running around like maniacs playing catch with somebody's pilfered baseball cap.

"So infantile," Mackenzie commented, chomping down on her pimento-avocado wrap from Zabar's delicatessen.

I had just finished the first half of my sun-dried tomato and mozzarella sandwich when we suddenly heard Timmy's raised voice coming from behind some poison oak trees and bushes on our left.

"Lay off me!" he was shouting. "It's my money, not yours! When are you going to get that through your thick skull?"

Mackenzie and I froze. We put down our food so we could listen better. Nothing like a little eavesdropping on a little verbal sparring to liven up a day in the woods.

"Don't talk to me like that! For God's sake, show me some respect!" came a woman's voice.

"Omigod!" Mackenzie said. "It's his weirdo mom!"

Mrs. Warner had come along with the other adult chaperones, but she didn't really seem to fit in with the other Westside parents. I mean, she usually dressed kind of shabbily, in old Costa Rican shawls and Kmart overalls, but almost on purpose, like she was making a point. She was kind of verbally crude, too—always laughing too loud, always going on about Timmy and his sister, and how they were going to be famous film actors.

"I can't believe Timmy talks to her like that!" Mackenzie murmured.

"Pretty rude," I agreed. "But not really out of character."

"Why should I respect you?" Timmy said bitterly. "You're nothing but a moneygrubbing witch!"

"You ingrate!" Mrs. Warner replied in a tear-filled

voice. "Who was it who got you into show business in the first place?"

"Hey, if you were any kind of a mother, you'd be delirious that your son was making good bucks!" he shot back.

"While I have to go around in rags? And what about your sister? Don't you think she could use a few dollars once in a while?"

"Marina can take care of herself," Timmy said. "Look, I've got to think of my future."

"I *am* thinking about your future! Do you know what kind of song and dance I had to do to get you a full scholarship to Westside?" Mrs. Warner asked, her voice rising again.

"I was the one who got the scholarship, not you," Timmy pointed out. "And if I took money out of my trust, don't you think the school would notice? That lousy scholarship would be gone in a minute!" Their voices grew fainter as they headed away, in the direction of the Falls Trail.

We didn't hear anything after that, because just then Ms. Conlan spotted us. "Are you two eating *already*?" she asked in a disapproving voice. "Come on, now, we need you for the volleyball game!" Mackenzie and I protested but she wasn't taking no for an answer.

In between points, I kept glancing over toward the trail head, expecting to see Timmy and his mom. Instead, I saw one of our demented classmates, Ernie

Zulia, sneaking off through the forsythia bushes. Now, that's weird, I thought. Maybe Ernie hadn't forgotten Timmy shutting him in his locker last week. I chuckled, imagining Ernie getting his revenge by pushing Timmy into the river. Not likely. Ernie was about half Timmy's size. Probably Ernie was just being nosy, I told myself. Even nosier than Mackenzie and me, apparently.

All the good psycho athletes were on one volleyball team, and as usual, Mackenzie and I were on the other. We got creamed two games in a row. Finally, our third defeat was declared a mercy killing, and we all broke for lunch.

The junior class gathered into its usual cliques—the jocks at one end of the picnic area, the freakazoids and goths at the other. Free spirits like Mackenzie and me scattered at various tables in between.

Walter Wenke plopped himself down between us. Walter is this really skinny kid who, unbelievably, wins the pie-eating contest every single year. This time, he pulled out a disgusting-looking sandwich on a poppy-seed bun. It was totally gross, oozing mayo from both sides as if the sandwich had mad cow disease.

"Ugh, Walter, get out of here with that!" Mackenzie groaned. "It makes me want to hurl just looking at it. How can you eat that?"

"It's *tongue*!" Walter said with a happy shrug, as if that explained everything. Then he chowed down, taking an enormous bite that made gobs of mayo drip onto the wooden table. That's Walter for you: the social skills of a rabid aardvark.

"I am *so* not hungry," Mackenzie moaned. "Thank you, Walter."

Fortunately, many years of school cafeteria experience have allowed me to eat no matter what revolting things are happening around me. I had just polished off the second half of my sandwich, and was getting up to leave the table, when we all heard the scream.

It was shrill and bloodcurdling. And it came from pretty far away—in the direction of the Falls Trail.

Before we could even start running, we heard a shrieking voice that was instantly recognizable as Mrs. Warner's. "Timmy! Oh, God, Timmy! Help! He's in the river! Oh, my God!"

Another scream followed, a long, long wail. All eyes turned in the direction of the falls.

"There he is!" Mackenzie gasped, pointing. We all saw Timmy thrashing, floating down the rapids toward the falls. We all took off running, but we didn't get far. It was way too late to do any good. We jogged to a standstill, then watched frozen in horror as Timmy Warner went over the edge and hurtled screaming down into the maelstrom.

2

Corpus Delicti—*Not*

The air was filled with the sounds of horrified kids and chaperones. Mackenzie and I immediately ran back down the trail toward the parking lot, figuring Timmy would be carried downriver in that direction.

Even as I ran, I knew our chances of saving him were less than zero. Either he'd been dashed on that pile of rocks below the falls, or else, even worse, he'd been carried into the spillway, and sucked into the roaring steel turbines of the hydroelectric facility. Can you say, "Fishburgers?"

I reached the river's edge ahead of everybody else just in time to catch a glimpse of yellow T-shirt and blue designer jeans as Timmy disappeared into the tunnel of the hydro plant.

"*Nooo!*" I heard myself yelling—okay, screaming. I'm telling you, I couldn't help it. It was the most horrible thing I'd ever seen—or *imagined*. Because the worst part of all was picturing Timmy going through sharp metal blades spinning at hundreds of miles per hour. My knees went weak, as if I were being chopped up by proxy.

"Poor Timmy," I said, as Mackenzie and the others came up beside me.

"Did you see him?" she asked, terrified.

"He went down the spillway," I said, hardly able to believe it, even though I'd just witnessed it.

"*No!*" Mackenzie cried. Nearly everyone had tears in their eyes, and some of the girls and a few boys were openly sobbing. Timmy Warner may not have been the most popular kid at Westside, but none of us would have wished *this* on him. We wouldn't have wished it on our worst enemy.

Marty Connors, our class's resident cross-country track star, ran to alert a nearby park ranger. The ranger immediately took out his walkie-talkie and yelled something into it, but we all knew it was way too late.

We walked back up the hill in stony silence. In the picnic area, Timmy's mom was on the ground, in a screaming, writhing, grief-stricken heap.

"How could it have happened?" Mackenzie said, choking back sobs as we stood there, numb with shock and horror.

"Maybe he was showing off or something," I said.

"You've got to fish him out of there!" Mrs. Warner was shouting. "Oh, my baby, my poor sweet baby!"

"You've got to stay calm now, Meryl," Ms. Conlan told her. "The rangers are searching for him. They're doing everything they can."

"He's dead, isn't he? My boy is *dead*!" Mrs. Warner

collapsed to the ground again, heaving one gut-wrenching sob after another.

"What happened, Meryl?" Ms. Conlan asked her. "Can you tell us?"

"We were . . . we were standing by the side of the river . . . just where the rapids start . . . that lead to the falls. . . ." She had to stop every four or five words to gulp down some air between sobs. "He was skimming stones into the river . . . I told him not to get so close, but he just laughed . . . he was always so sure of himself." She sniffed back more tears, and her face crumpled as she said, "And then . . . he slipped. Oh God, my baby!"

That was it. She was off again, writhing on the ground, tearing at her hair and her face, sobbing and screaming incoherently. One of the parents, who was a well-known cardiac surgeon, fished a pill bottle out of his pocket and gave her two tablets. He explained, "She'll be okay in a little while."

A park ranger rode up the trail on a quad, driving with one hand and talking on his walkie-talkie with the other. He stepped forward and beckoned Ms. Conlan aside. They spoke in low tones, and Ms. Conlan gasped, her hand covering her mouth. Luckily, Mrs. Warner was too far gone to notice.

Then I looked up, and caught a glimpse of Ernie Zulia. He was half hidden behind a big oak tree, whose leaves had gone yellow but hadn't yet begun to fall. Ernie's eyes were hooded with some sort of dark, weird emotion. He was staring straight at Meryl Warner. His jaw was slack with something that wasn't grief, but looked more like—well, fear and horror.

"Back in a minute," I told Mackenzie, and went over to talk with him. "Hey, Ernie," I said. "You don't look so good."

"I'm okay," he said, staring at the ground.

"Come on, Ernie, I saw you follow the two of them up the trail. What did you see? What happened to Timmy?"

"I don't know!" he insisted. "I left before he fell in."

"But you *saw* something," I insisted. "Or *heard* something. I can see it in your eyes. Tell me, dude."

"I don't know. . . ."

I sighed impatiently. "Come on, Ernie! Timmy's probably chopped meat! Don't you realize what people are gonna think?"

"What?" Ernie's eyes suddenly bulged with fear. "Wh-what are they gonna think?"

"You had a grudge against Timmy, right? What, did you push him in or something?"

"I never went near him!" he wailed. "It was *her*, not me!"

I thought that one over a minute. "What are you saying, Ernie?"

"They were fighting, that's all. She shoved him, and I saw him slap her across the face, and then I sneezed. Timmy heard me, so I got out of there fast."

"And that was how long before he fell in?"

"I don't know. Five minutes, maybe."

I stared at him hard. "Do you realize what you're suggesting?"

"Only that they were fighting. I don't know. Maybe she pushed him again, and he was too close to the water. I don't know *what* to think!"

He broke free of me, and ran off to join the rest of the class.

Mackenzie zipped over to me. "That looked bizarre," she said.

"It was," I said. *"Very."*

3

The Merry Widow

There were *so* many things to think over. Several events had taken place after my little conversation with Ernie Zulia.

Timmy's shredded jeans and T-shirt were brought up for identification. They'd been retrieved from the turbines, and the sight of them sent Mrs. Warner into fresh hysterics. She was re-sedated, and taken away in an ambulance to Milford County Hospital for observation.

Timmy's body was not found—not even a trace of it. The police presumed it would have been sliced into little pieces, in which case, it would *never* be found.

Most interesting of all—when it was time to go, and we all grabbed our backpacks, Timmy Warner's came up missing. Ernie swore that Timmy didn't have it with him when he went up the trail with his mother. On the other hand, we'd all seen him take it off the bus and carry it to the picnic area. He'd had it with him when Mac and I saw him arguing with his mother. *So where was it?*

The police and park rangers figured it had gone over

the falls with Timmy. It would turn up sooner or later—unless it had been stolen. They said the park was crowded with hikers this time of year and some of them were prone to take things that didn't belong to them.

That was possible, but something told me it wasn't what had happened. Mackenzie's got chills on the top of her head, a sure sign she agreed with me (she always gets these chills when something's wrong). I admit that I have a suspicious nature, but I was positive something fishy had happened right under our noses.

It was two hours later when we finally got back on the school bus for the long ride home. Timmy's seat remained eerily empty. Mackenzie sat with me. Mary Beckinsall, who'd sat next to me on the way, moved up beside Ms. Conlan in exchange for a bribe—a pack of Choco-Chews Mackenzie had in her backpack.

Mackenzie and I didn't talk much on the ride, though. We knew better than to air our theories in front of our classmates. Speculating on the nature of Timmy's death so soon might have also been viewed as somewhat insensitive.

Halloween in New York City is not to be believed. There's the mega-freak parade that goes up Sixth Avenue in Greenwich Village and ends up in Washington Square Park. The costumes are as glitzy and demented as at Mardi Gras in New Orleans. Last year one woman was on stilts and dressed as a thirty-five-foot lobster. There was a sixty-foot fire-breathing dragon, and the Brothers of the Acropolis rode a float in the shape of the Winged Victory. A couple of teenagers were dressed as pretzels, and one model wore a giant hat with a live poodle in it. But the parade is just the start of it. There are parties everywhere and the streets are filled with ghouls, dead celebrities, aliens, and vampires.

Mackenzie and I had planned a couple of awesome costumes for the three parties we'd been invited to. We figured we'd fiesta-hop from one to the other, me as Leonardo DiCaprio in *Titanic* after he's drowned; Mackenzie as the Kate Winslet character at the end, when she's a hundred years old.

Mackenzie had made most of her costume herself, being short of money as usual. Me, I'd just gone cheapo shopping, but I have to say I was pleased with the results. The chalky blue of my skin was totally realistic, not to mention the amazing resemblance between me and Leonardo—ha-ha. Anyway, Halloween was less than a week away and the closer it got, the more Timmy Warner as steak tartare was on everybody's mind.

As the park ranges had predicted, Timmy's body had not been found. So on October twentieth, three weeks after the accident, he'd been declared "presumed dead." A memorial service was set for the twenty-fifth at West Side Memorial Chapel. I'd been there once or twice before, for funerals of old people, but never for a kid.

Inside, a few rows of benches had been set aside for

the kids and parents who were on the outing. Not that anyone had been all that crazy about Timmy—but you know how it is. When someone dies, particularly in such a horrible way, and so young, you tend to forget the bad and remember the good.

Mackenzie was no different. In spite of the fact that she'd practically detested Timmy, now she was all remorse and regret. "Maybe I should have gone out with him," she said, sniffing back tears as we pushed through the crowd to find our seats. "He liked me so much . . . and all I did was reject him."

"Mackenzie, he was a *jerk*, remember?" I said as delicately as I could. "It's okay that you didn't like him."

"I shouldn't have been so mean to him," she insisted. "I could have given him a little happiness in his short life . . . just by saying yes. . . ."

"Are you nuts?" I said.

I sighed as we took our seats. No point in arguing logically with revisionist history at that moment.

"He was just lonely," she said, shaking her head. "Poor Timmy. All he wanted was to fit in with everybody else. He couldn't afford expensive clothes like most of the kids . . . I can identify with that. . . ."

"He dressed okay," I whispered. "Those shredded jeans were Tommy Hilfigers, I noticed."

"They were his best pair," she countered. "And he wore them all the time."

"He had loot," I insisted. "From all those commercials."

"Yes, but he was always bellyaching about how he couldn't touch it without losing his scholarship, remember?" she said. "Who knows? He might have been making half of everything up. Truth was never one of his strong cards."

The organ started to play Timmy's favorite Bee Gee songs from *Saturday Night Fever*. It was a music selection totally in line with Mrs. Warner's flair for the inappropriate.

"Where's his mom?" I whispered. "Anybody seen her?" I looked around at the other kids in our section, but all I got were shrugs and shakes of the head.

And then, the murmuring started. It was like a wave of sound emanating from the back of the chapel. Mourners fell back, gasping at the vision in black that had entered the hall, and was loudly sobbing her way down the center aisle toward the altar. It sort of *looked* like Timmy's mom, but this new Mrs. Meryl Warner had been totally transformed.

"Get a load of *her*!" Mackenzie murmured in astonishment, echoing the rest of the crowd. The new, improved, glamorous Mrs. Warner was dressed in a black silk designer dress—cut more for evening wear than funeral wear, if you ask me. She also wore large diamond stud earrings, and carried an alligator bag that must have cost hundreds of dollars.

"I wonder who did her hair?" Mackenzie said into my ear. "It's definitely salon cut, I'll tell you that much."

Now, you have to understand something. The Meryl Warner we'd all come to know was a tired-looking woman in her early forties, sporting tacky discount-store threads. This new version was not what anybody was expecting—not by a long shot.

"She must have struck gold or something," Mackenzie remarked.

"Maybe she came into an inheritance," I suggested.

"You mean . . . ?"

"I sure would like to know who Timmy had down as the beneficiary of his trust fund."

"Are you suggesting what I think you are?" Mackenzie said.

"I'm not suggesting anything," I said with a shrug. "But it is kind of curious, you've got to admit."

"Curious is not the word," she said, folding her arms across her chest. "It's like she's telling all the other parents, 'See? I'm one of you now, and I don't care what you think!'"

"Hey, what do you say we do a little nosing around, and see what we can find out?"

"Right now?"

"Mmm, I guess you're right. That would be kind of disrespectful to Timmy's memory," I pointed out.

"I suppose," she concurred. "Okay. How 'bout right after?"

"You're on," I said.

4

The Sweet Smell of Rat

It's hard to get your brain around the notion that a mother might have actually killed her own child. The sad fact is this sort of thing does occasionally happen. And Timmy's mom showing up at the memorial service looking like Ivana Trump, while it might not mean anything in itself, was enough to make me and Mackenzie wonder.

After the service, knots of kids and parents milled around in the Indian-summer sunshine on Amsterdam Avenue. Everyone was talking about Timmy, and especially about Mrs. Warner, who had left immediately after the service in a stretch limo.

"I think we should pay her a visit ASAP," Mackenzie said, as we watched the limo glide away into traffic.

"Do we even know where Timmy lived?" I asked, realizing that I, for one, had no idea. He'd never thrown a party, probably because his acting money was all tied up in his trust fund and he couldn't afford to. In any case, if he had thrown any parties, *I* sure hadn't been invited.

"I don't have a clue," Mackenzie said with a shrug. "We could ask one of his friends."

"Yeah? Like who?"

"Mmm. Good point."

"I guess we could look him up in the book," I suggested.

"Great! Let's do it," Mackenzie said.

"Uh, you go ahead," I told her. "There's something else I have to do first."

Mackenzie followed my gaze. It was fixed on Ernie Zulia, who was huddled alone against the front of the funeral parlor, lost in his own brooding thoughts.

"Ah. I get it," Mackenzie said. "But how 'bout *you* go look up his address, and *I* worm the juicy stuff out of Ernie?"

"It was my idea," I pointed out.

Mackenzie made a face. "Okay, you win. I'll meet you at the corner of Columbus Avenue when you're done, and we can head over to the Warners'."

Mackenzie raced off down the street to find a diner with an intact Manhattan white pages. I turned toward my prey, and walked over to him. Ernie looked up at me with terror in his eyes.

"*What?*" he asked. He must have had a fair idea of what I wanted. From the looks of him, he either had a very guilty conscience, or he was sitting on some pretty important information.

"Spill it, Ernie," I said. "You might as well tell me

right now. You know you're going to eventually."

"Who says?" he said belligerently.

"Of course, you could always tell your story to the police. I hear they have some very nice holding cells for suspects. . . ."

"*Suspects?*" Beads of sweat broke out on Ernie's forehead, and trickled down between his zits. "What are you talking about? I already told you what I heard up there on the trail!"

"The *rest* of it, Ernie," I demanded. "The whole enchilada."

Ernie crumbled like a stale cookie. "Well," he said, in a voice so low that only I could hear it. "As I told you, they were fighting over Timmy's money."

"And . . . ?"

"Well, she wanted him to make it over to her . . . and he said no, the lawyers were in charge of it, and they'd warned him not to let her go anywhere near it."

"Uh-huh . . ."

"And then . . ." His voice trailed off. I waited. "And then . . ."

"You said that was when you sneezed," I reminded him.

"Yeah, but not right then . . . first, Timmy said something about a policy."

"Policy?" My ears pricked up. "What kind of policy?"

"Insurance, I think. A life-insurance policy his mom had taken out on him . . . or something like that. It was hard to hear!" Ernie insisted.

"I'm sure it was. But Ernie, you have very good hearing."

"Um, thanks," he said, not sure whether I was being sincere. "Anyway, Timmy said something like, 'You'd be happier if I was dead, wouldn't you?'"

"Aha. And?"

"Well, she denied it all over the place, but he just kept coming at her with it. I think he'd found the policy in her drawer or something, and he was pretty ticked off."

"And?"

"And . . . that's when I sneezed. Really! It is!"

"Okay, Ernie," I said with a sigh. "I believe you. Thanks a bunch."

I turned to leave. "Hey!" he stopped me. "What about the police?"

"Oh, yeah," I said. "Leave it to me, okay?" I gave him a thumbs-up, and he broke out into a stainless-steel smile. Then I went looking for Mackenzie.

Half an hour later, just as I finished filling Mackenzie in on my interview with Ernie, our cab pulled up in front of the Warners' building—a twelve-story, prewar job that had seen better days, and hadn't yet benefitted from the city's real-estate boom.

"Egad," I said, using one of my trademark expressions. "Doesn't quite go with the stretch limo, does it?"

"Not by a long shot," Mackenzie agreed, paying the cabbie and joining me on the sidewalk.

Let's just say this was not a doorman building, okay?

There was, however, a wall full of doorbells in the vestibule, and Mackenzie ran her fingers down them until she found WARNER 12C. She rang the bell, and we waited for Timmy's mom's voice to come through the intercom.

There was no answer. We tried twice more, but got the same result. "Maybe we should ring the super," I suggested.

In buildings like this one, supers usually know everything that goes on. But apparently the super was gone, too—out to lunch, literally or figuratively. So Mackenzie and I went back outside, and leaned against the building.

Mackenzie looked troubled. "What is it?" I asked her.

"Something isn't right," she said. "I've got chills on the top of my head."

Mackenzie's scalp is never wrong.

"Think we should wait around?" I asked.

"I don't know." She bit her lip, staring into space. Then she quickly turned to me. "P.C., where would Timmy's mom have gone right after a funeral—other than home?"

"Beats me."

"No place, that's where. There's no cemetery where he's buried. And you don't typically go out and party after a memorial service. It's not natural."

"Yeah? So?"

Her eyes lit up. "Remember what Ernie told you?

What if she killed Timmy, got the insurance money, and took off for Mexico or someplace so the law couldn't touch her?"

I cleared my throat. "Sounds kinda speculative. I mean, it's a theory, but I don't know. . . ."

"It makes sense, though, doesn't it? I'll bet she's already skipped town with the money. . . ."

"Mackenzie," I said, "If you're right, and she's in Mexico with her blood money, there's not a whole lot we can do about it."

Mackenzie frowned. "I guess you're right."

"Why don't we just hang around awhile and see if she comes back?"

"You mean, just stand here and do nothing?"

"Well, we could sit in the window of that coffee shop across the street and have a bite to eat. Hey, while we're at it, we could check out whether there really is an insurance policy—and whether it's already been paid out."

"Good idea," she agreed. "Why don't we ask Jesus?"

Mackenzie didn't mean anything religious; she was talking about our friend and computer guru, Jesus Lopez. He lives in a brownstone on the corner of West 73rd and Riverside Drive, and he gets around in a wheelchair better than most kids do on two feet.

He's only thirteen years old (he's a freshman at Westside), but he's the best computer hacker I've ever run across. Tracking down a life insurance policy was a job tailor-made for Jesus.

"Good idea," I told Mackenzie. "Give him a buzz."

She whipped out her cell phone (you notice she's not too poor to have a cell phone, which, by the way, her parents pay for) and speed-dialed Jesus' number. "Hey, you," she said into the flip-down mouthpiece. "We need you to do a little snooping for us. Are you up for it?"

Mackenzie gave Jesus a quick run-down of what we needed. Then we went across the street and over to the Green Kitchen for some eggs Benedict. In Mackenzie's case, eggs Florentine (Benedict with spinach instead of bacon). She's a somewhat healthier eater than I am. Anyway, we'd barely polished off our home fries when her cell phone started playing "Take Me Out to the Ballgame."

I picked it up before Mackenzie could grab it. "Hello?"

"Yo, I got you the name of the insurance company," Jesus said. Nobody can hack like Jesus, and I mean *nobody*. "It's Northeast Mutual—and the amount of the policy—get this—is three million dollars!"

I nearly choked on the last mouthful of my eggs. "How much?!"

"You heard me, dude. Oh, and hey, it just so happens the same company is in charge of the kid's trust fund through their brokerage house. Just so you know, the money goes to his sister, not his mother."

"Oh, yeah? How much was in the trust fund?"

"Two fifty."

"Two hundred fifty thousand?"

"That's what I said."

"Sheesh!" Timmy had obviously done better as an actor than I'd thought.

Mackenzie and I paid the check, and raced out of there as fast as we could. Northeast Mutual was down on Madison Avenue and 23rd Street. Normally, we would have taken the Lexington Avenue subway, but it was getting on into the afternoon, and we didn't want to wait until after school the following day. Something freakazoid was going on with Mrs. Warner, and if we wanted to get to the bottom of this case, we were going to have to be as fast as she was.

Disappearing Act

The Northeast Mutual Life Building is one of those old New York City landmarks you see lit up on every postcard shot of the nighttime skyline. It looks kind of like an upturned pencil with a luminous golden tip. There's even a commercial with film footage from the 1920s, showing men building it.

Whatever. The point is, even though you grow up in Manhattan, you never actually go into any of these buildings, until one day, you have a specific, weird reason to be there—or unless, of course, you have visitors from out of town who want to see every tourist attraction in the guidebook.

We rode the elevator up to the forty-third floor. After waiting in the reception area for an obscenely long time, we were shown into the office of Mr. Clement Hall, the agent who was handling the Warner policy.

Mr. Hall looked like he'd stepped right out of a TV soap opera. He was plasticky handsome. He had a perfect, capped-teeth smile, and eyes that were so blue he had to be wearing colored contact lenses. His hair was gelled into place, and wouldn't have moved even if a tornado had struck. His voice, when he spoke, was an actor's smooth baritone, with perfect pitch and no trace of any accent.

"Well, hello there, kids," he said, stretching his lips around his smile even further. "Sit down. What can I do for you today?"

I hate when people call us *kids* in that tone that makes it sound like we're baby goats. I already hated this guy. I could tell he wasn't going to take us seriously, and he hadn't even heard us out yet.

Nevertheless, I forged ahead. "We're here about the life insurance policy Meryl Warner took out on her son Timmy."

His face darkened into a mask of sorrow. "Ah, yes. What a terrible tragedy."

For a minute, I wondered what he was talking about—Timmy's death or the company's losing a few million dollars. But then he continued, "Such a promising young man, I understand. I never met him, of course, but I did speak with Mrs. Warner afterward. She was terribly upset, understandably so."

"Mmm," I grunted. Mackenzie always tells me not to grunt so much. But what can I tell you? I'm a grunter, always have been, probably always will be. Besides, grunting can be an asset. In this case, for instance, Mr. Hall took it for sympathy. "Did you kids know Timmy well?" he asked.

Every time he called us *kids*, I found my fists clenching involuntarily.

"Pretty well," Mackenzie said. "Mr. Hall, we're here because we think there might have been foul play."

His eyes registered shock, but his voice remained perfectly modulated. "Foul play? Are you—do you have any—I mean, what makes you say that?"

I recounted the argument we'd overheard and also the one Ernie Zulia had told us about. I also mentioned Mrs. Warner's attire and attitude at the memorial service.

Hall nodded slowly, but seemed unimpressed. "Look," he said, as if he were talking to a pair of cretins, "I understand how this whole thing must have upset you. It's unnatural, in and of itself, for a young person in perfect health to die. And in such a sudden, horrible way. It's completely normal for dark suspicions to come into young, imaginative minds."

"Haven't you even listened to a word we've said?" I asked, hoping I didn't look as irritated as I felt.

"Of course I have," Hall countered, oozing calm and scorn at the same time. "You're suggesting this mother murdered her own child for money, isn't that right?"

Hearing it put that way kind of took me aback. "Well, um, yeah," I agreed. "I guess we are suggesting that."

"A little extreme, don't you think? A bit of a reach?"

"But—she took out a policy on her son worth three million dollars! Don't you think that's a little unusual?"

"It's hardly unusual for a parent to take out a

multi-million-dollar policy on a child who has the potential to bring in a large income. We've got some parents of kids who play their guitar in a club for one night and they think they're well on their way to becoming a rock star. A million dollars barely buys a family's cars these days. You'd be surprised at the number of parents who think they've just popped out the next Michael Jordan or Britney Spears. And sure, parents and teenagers fight about money. We've seen fistfights here at the office. I understand there may have been money troubles and conflicts in the Warner home. Nothing unusual about that."

He put a hand on my shoulder. I wanted to bite it off.

"Perhaps it would interest you to know," Mackenzie said, "that Mrs. Warner has already changed her lifestyle. She showed up at the funeral in a gold stretch limo, wearing diamonds and expensive clothes. She did a lot of dramatic sobbing, but she looked awfully good doing it."

Hall gave Mackenzie a sad smile. "Often, the grief of losing a child is overwhelming to a parent. The insurance money must have caused Mrs. Warner a lot of pain, coming as it did as compensation for Timmy's loss. It wouldn't be at all surprising—psychologically speaking—if she felt compelled to go out and spend some of it extravagantly, even wastefully. It's ironic, but shopping often has a way of soothing great grief."

Mackenzie backed down, slumping in her chair. I could tell she silently agreed with the shopping theory.

It didn't matter. We weren't going to get this guy to believe anything we said.

"Look," Hall continued, "we paid Mrs. Warner very quickly, it's true. Normally, we wait until the body has been found and the cause of death certified by the coroner. But in this case, Timmy's death was witnessed by at least forty people, all of whom saw him fall down the spillway into the turbines. His clothes were found in shreds. There wouldn't have been much of poor Timmy left to find."

Hearing Hall tell the story of Timmy's fall brought the horrific image back to me. Also, his explanation of Mrs. Warner's behavior did make sense, sort of.

"Look, if we did find out it was murder, it would be to this company's benefit," Hall pointed out. "We would recover our three million dollars. Believe me when I tell you we don't pay out easily. If there was any real evidence of foul play, we'd be very interested to receive it. But your suspicions are just that, I'm afraid—suspicions. Without concrete evidence, there's nothing we can do."

He ushered us to the door. "Anyway, thank you for coming to see us. We appreciate your desire to help. And it was a pleasure meeting you."

Mackenzie and I had barely stepped into the hallway when the office door clicked shut.

"Ugh, I need a shower," Mackenzie said, shuddering. "What a slimy, patronizing man!"

As we turned the corner, we almost bumped into a

young guy in a gray suit. "Oh—sorry," he said. "I, um, couldn't help overhearing . . . you know, if you *did* find out it was murder, there's a twenty-five-thousand-dollar reward."

"What?!" Mackenzie snapped to attention.

"Twenty-five thousand," the guy repeated. "It's standard—the reward clause is built into all the policies we write. Believe me, it's worth it to us—cuts back on insurance fraud."

"Twenty-five thousand!" she repeated, her eyes widening. "Come on, P.C.—we've got some investigating to do!"

We rode the subway back uptown. It was past six o'clock by now, and the car was crammed with fermenting rush-hour commuters. We could barely breathe, let alone talk. By the time we got out at 86th and Lexington, it was already getting dark.

"Mrs. Warner ought to be home by now," Mackenzie said, her blond hair fanned out behind her as she ran down the street. "We've got to question her, P.C. If she's got a guilty conscience, we'll know it. It'll be written all over her face."

We turned the corner of Mrs. Warner's block—and stopped in our tracks. There, in front of the building, was a big moving van, its motor running. Two big, burly guys were just closing the rear doors and pulling up the metal ramp.

"P.C.!" Mackenzie gasped.

"Mackenzie, if that's Mrs. Warner's stuff, I think you should start your own psychic hotline. Come on!"

We ran, waving at the two guys, who were just getting into the cab of the van. "Wait! Wait!" we shouted.

But it was too late. The engine roared to life, and the van pulled out into traffic. We ran down the street after it—but it just barely made the light, and we had to stop or be flattened by the taxis racing up and down York Avenue.

"Dang!" Mackenzie gasped, bending over to catch her breath.

"Maybe it wasn't Mrs. Warner's stuff," I suggested.

"Come on," she said. "Let's go see."

We rang Mrs. Warner's bell, but as before, there was no answer. Then we tried the super's bell.

A chubby Latino lady came to the door, a squeegee in one hand and a smile on her face. "Yes?" she asked.

"Ma'am, can you tell us who those movers were here for?"

"Oh, that's Mrs. Warner," she said, a sad look coming over her face. "Poor lady."

"She's moving out?"

"She already left this afternoon," the super told us. "She going to California—Los Angeles."

"Do you know her new address?" Mackenzie asked.

"Sorry," the lady shrugged. "She say she don't know yet where she gonna be. She wanna be near her daughter, I think. You know, the loco one."

"Here's our number," Mackenzie said, scribbling it on a piece of paper and handing it to the lady. "If you find out where Mrs. Warner's staying, could you let us know?"

The super looked at us with suspicion. "You friends of Timmy?" she asked.

"That's right," I said quickly. "Good friends."

"'Cause he and his mama no like each other—they fight all the time, like every day. Yelling, screaming . . . I think he throw things against the wall. He got a temper."

"Really?" I said. "What were they fighting about?"

"Oh, I don't know nothing," the lady said. "These old buildings you can't hear much. But they was yelling and screaming a lot. You sure you was friends with Timmy?"

"Oh, yeah," Mackenzie said. "He told us his mom wanted his money or something."

"Yeah, I hear that too," the lady said, giving us a little crooked smile. "I don't think she too happy with him. But she got lotsa dough now. Too bad she got no son. Only that show-biz daughter." She shook her head and started sweeping the vestibule.

Mackenzie motioned to me that it was time for us to go.

"So," I asked her as we walked back toward the subway. "Are you up for a little trip to the West Coast?"

Mackenzie looked at me, outraged. "What do you mean, am I up for it? I'm *there*!"

6

La-La Land

Getting permission to take off across the continent on a moment's notice, on what seemed like a wild-goose chase, was easier than you might think. First of all, our parents are globe-trotters themselves—except for Mackenzie's mom, who is a New York City coroner, and is usually buried four stories underground with a gaggle of cadavers at the forensics lab downtown.

Besides, our parents know we're capable of taking care of ourselves. We do it all the time when they go away. We're experienced travelers in our own right, too. Between us, we've been to Borneo, the Congo, New Guinea, the Faroe Islands, and Cincinnati, just to mention some of the wilder places. So the urban jungle of L.A. seemed pretty tame by comparison.

To make a long story short, Westside School agreed to let us take a week's worth of classwork and homework to do on our own (our grades are generally pretty good). Our school is always making exceptions for the students. Last year Helen Kazan got two months off to tour Japan in a production of *The Sound of Music* starring

Debby Boone. My dad even gave us some of his millions of frequent-flyer miles. He called my uncle Dave—my mom's younger brother, who lives in L.A. and shoots commercials for a living—and asked him to let us crash with him for a few days. Uncle Dave is pretty cool, and was unfazed by the short notice. He said he'd meet us at LAX (that's the Los Angeles airport, in case you've never been there), and put us up at his garden apartment in Santa Monica.

And so, the following Thursday morning, Mackenzie and I settled into our seats on the 737, heading west in search of another mystery—or rather, in search of Mrs. Meryl Warner and her weird daughter, Marina.

My mission was to solve a murder—if a murder had been committed—or at the very least, to put my suspicions to rest. I was beginning to think that Mackenzie's mission had more to do with landing the $25,000 reward from the insurance company.

Once we were airborne, she started right in talking about how she was going to spend her share. "I've got to start shopping in a better class of store," she said. "No more encore shops. And ooooh, have you seen those new scooters with the electric motors? Picture me getting around town on one of those, P.C."

"Mackenzie, they cost like six hundred dollars, unless you get one of the rip-off models where the handlebars fall off."

"So? Think of all the cab fares and subway fares I'll

save. It'll probably pay for itself in a few months."

"Yeah," I said with a grin. "I can just picture you zigzagging your way through rush-hour traffic."

She didn't catch the note of sarcasm in my voice. "Right! They are so cool, aren't they?"

I had to admit they were. The scooter wasn't the end of it, though. Mackenzie was just getting started.

"I think we should throw a party, too—you know, invite every kid in the school, even the freakazoid ones we can't stand—just to show there are no hard feelings."

"This party . . . it's gonna be at your house, right?" I asked.

"We'll rent out a club or something. Yeah, with a really hot deejay!"

Let her have her fantasy, I figured. And besides, I knew Mackenzie too well to think she would blow all her reward money on the kids at school. She'd watch her loot like a hawk, just as she always did.

The plane landed, and Mac and I grabbed our gear. We stepped out of the airport baggage claim, and into the brilliant Southern California sunshine. "Whoa!" I said. "Time to bag this sweater."

"Thanks for letting us stay with you, Dave," Mackenzie said as Uncle Dave lugged her overstuffed duffle bag to his car.

"No prob," he said. "I'm looking forward to having you guys around. I warn you, though, L.A. is addictive—you're never going to want to leave."

Obviously, my uncle Dave is a big L.A. fan. You would be, too, if you'd been hanging out with B and C list actors and directors and screenwriters and models for the last ten years. He's got a pretty cool life.

I'll tell you, I was already halfway sold on the place myself. That morning, we'd left New York in twenty-degree weather. Now, here we were among the bougainvillea and palm trees, enjoying the warm breeze. Okay, so maybe the air smelled of smog—but never mind that. Uncle Dave says the air quality is getting better every year, and who am I to argue?

"Wow! A classic sixty-five Mustang convertible!" Mackenzie exclaimed when she saw Uncle Dave's car. "This is yours?"

"Actually, it's mostly the auto finance company's," Dave joked, as we got in and he took the top down. "But I get to drive it, and that's what counts."

Dave and the Mustang were a strange pair, if you ask me. Okay, they're about the same age. But that's where the resemblance ends. The Mustang is sleek and hot, while Dave is short, chubby, and balding. I guess you could say they both wear their hair down—Dave's, what there is of it, is in a ponytail, and the Mustang's top comes down with the push of a button.

I guess Dave's dream is that some starlet or model will see him behind the wheel of his Mustang and mistake him for Eminem or Brad Pitt. Not gonna happen—but you can't fault Dave for trying. As the New York Lotto ad says, You gotta be in it to win it.

"Where are we headed first?" I asked as we drove toward the airport exit.

"I thought I'd take you guys down Rodeo Drive," Dave said. "That's the main shopping drag in Beverly Hills. The home of conspicuous consumption."

"Sounds like nirvana to me!" Mackenzie said with a sigh, sitting back and letting the breeze play with her hair. With her mirrored shades and her blissed-out smile, she looked like an Angeleno already.

"You're going to torture us with all the fancy stuff we can't afford, is that it?" I teased Dave.

"Can't afford *yet*," Mackenzie corrected, biting her lip.

We oooed and aaahed our way through Beverly Hills—Spago, Louis Vuitton, Gucci. That inspired Uncle Dave to take us past some of the stars' houses in Beverly Hills. Lucille Ball's place, Jimmy Stewart's house (when they were alive). The Playboy Mansion. Streisand's digs. "I thought I'd take you over to the Sunset Strip for lunch where stars sometimes hang out."

"I could eat," I said, nodding.

"*Fab-u!*" Mackenzie chimed in.

"Great!" Dave enthused, and gunned the engine.

"Cameron Diaz and Leonardo DiCaprio are part-owners of this place," Dave told us as we dug into our veggie wraps.

I had to admit, the Standard Hotel was pretty cool. There were chairs in the lobby that were suspended from the ceiling, and you could swing on them. There was a pool in the back, where the young and mostly European guests sat baking themselves in suntan oil. Everything in the hotel was designed by the hippest, hottest designers—Dave said it was typical L.A., and that we should see it late at night—or no, on second thought, maybe we shouldn't, since we were too young.

Over lunch, while Mackenzie kept craning her neck to try to spot someone famous, I told Dave the story of how we came to be visiting L.A. He seemed fascinated. I don't think it had ever really registered with him that I was a "budding detective," as he put it.

"So where does this chick live?" he asked, meaning Mrs. Warner. I've gotta tell you, I had a hard time thinking of Mrs. Warner as a "chick." At best, she was a hen.

"We don't know yet," I explained. "We're waiting for a call from our pal Jesus."

"He's tracking her down on the Internet," Mackenzie explained.

"When do you think he'll let you know?" Dave asked.

"He said by the end of the business day, New York time," I said.

"That's right about now," Dave said, his eyes on the designer wall clock in the shape of a gondola. And wouldn't you know it, right on time, Mackenzie's cell phone went off.

"Hello," she said, whipping out her pad and pen. "Okay, shoot." She wrote down the address. "Go Jesus—you're the best!" she said, hanging up.

"Resourceful *and* prompt," Dave remarked. "Let's see what you've got there." He took the pad and studied the address. "Hmm . . ." he said. "This place is in Toluca Lake, up near Burbank. I've got a commercial shoot up that way at four. How about I drop you off where you're going, then meet you around six. I should be done by then."

"Sounds like a plan," I agreed.

And that was how we came to be in Toluca Lake as the sun set over the Hollywood Hills. Dave left us in front of the Falcon Theatre, an old movie house that had been turned into a venue for live stage shows. We'd agreed to meet across from there, at the original Bob's Big Boy Restaurant, at six.

"Okay," Mackenzie said, studying the street map we'd bought along the way. "According to this, we're only three blocks away from Mrs. Warner's."

"Good. Well, here we go!" I said, feeling more energized than I'd felt all day. Nothing like a case of possible murder to get my juices flowing.

It was dark as we rounded a corner and found ourselves in front of Mrs. Warner's apartment complex. It was a pink building, three stories high, with walkways running the length of it on each floor. Kind of like a motel, with shrubs in front lit up by colored lights.

"She's in apartment two-fourteen," Mackenzie read from her notebook.

"Must be temporary quarters, until she finds herself a better pad in Beverly Hills," I remarked.

We went up a flight of stairs and down the walkway in the darkness until we were in front of the door marked 214. There was no sound, except for thousands of crickets doing their thing in the bushes below, and the noises of cars in the distance, going up and down the boulevard.

"Should we knock?" Mackenzie whispered.

"I don't know. What do you think?"

Just then, we heard screaming from inside the apartment! It was Mrs. Warner, all right. She sounded the same as she had on the afternoon Timmy went over the falls.

"Timmy! Timmy, I know it's you! Say something! Timmy, please! Talk to me! Timmy! Timmeeee!"

7

Trouble in Mind

I know Mackenzie is the one who usually gets chills on the top of her head. But believe me, at that moment, every cell in my body was frozen.

Was Timmy in that room, on the other side of that closed apartment door? And if so, was he alive? I don't really believe in ghosts, but Mrs. Warner sounded exactly like someone who did.

What in the world was happening here?

It took a long moment for us both to recover our wits. Mackenzie crept closer to the door, and planted her ear to it so she could hear better. I noticed that the big picture window next to the door was covered by thick white curtains on the inside, but that there was a small crack between the drapes. I tiptoed over to that crack, glued my eyeball to the glass, and cupped my hands around my face. After a second or two, the picture in the darkened living room began to come clear before my eyes.

Mrs. Warner was on the phone, still screaming and sobbing. "Oh my God, I'm going crazy!" she was jabbering, all the time hyperventilating as she paced back and forth. "Are you trying to drive me out of my mind, is that it? Timmy, answer me! I know it's you!" Finally, she gave up, and with a last, long, loud wail, threw the phone against the wall. She collapsed on the couch, sobbing and tearing at her hair.

"Oh . . . my . . . God . . ." Mackenzie whispered to me. I motioned for her to come see what I was seeing. The two of us stared through the little gap in the curtains, watching Mrs. Warner go into the fetal position on the sofa, moaning and weeping.

After a minute or so, she calmed down, and picked up the phone again. She pushed the talk button to see if it was still working. Apparently satisfied that it was, she took out a gargantuan yellow pages and started thumbing through it. When she'd found what she was looking for, she punched in the number and waited.

I could feel Mackenzie's breathing, hear her heart pounding as we stood there, inches apart. If someone else had left their apartment and come out onto the walkway at that moment, we would have looked mad suspicious, I can tell you that.

"Hello!" Mrs. Warner breathed into the phone. We could barely hear her, now that she wasn't ranting and raving so much. "I need a home consultation. I don't care what it costs."

Mackenzie and I shot each other a puzzled look.

"All right—if you must know—" Mrs. Warner continued,

"I think my son may be trying to contact me . . . from . . . from the other side."

"Whoa," Mackenzie mouthed to me.

Mrs. Warner listened, then said, "A séance? Well, if you think that will work . . . but don't we need a certain number of people for that?" She listened again. "I see. Well, possibly. I'll have to think about it . . . what time could you be here? Oh, right. Yes, of course, I can understand it has to be after dark. Eight o'clock tomorrow will be fine. Yes. Thank you so much." She ended the call, and collapsed back onto the couch.

I straightened up to stretch. I hadn't realized it, but I'd been bent over in such a weird position for so long that my left leg was asleep. Trying to shake it off, I bumped into Mackenzie, who was still peering through the window. Her head butted the glass so hard I thought the window would break.

As it was, the noise was enough to alert Mrs. Warner. "Timmy, is that you?" she cried out, and I could imagine how fast she'd sprung up from the couch. "Timmy! Stop haunting me!"

I thought I could hear her footsteps heading for the apartment door, as Mackenzie and I ran for the stairs—with me hopping on the one leg I could feel. We were halfway down the flight of steps when we heard the door being flung open. "Timmy! I know you're out here!" Mrs. Warner yelled into the night.

"Keep it down, lady!" someone shouted from another

apartment. "I'm tryin' to watch TV in here!"

Mackenzie and I stood frozen against the pink stucco wall of the staircase, not even daring to breathe, let alone move. We knew that if Mrs. Warner came down the stairs, she'd find us, but there was nothing else we could do. If we ran for it, we'd be caught in the decorative lighting on the walkway and bushes in front of the building. The best we could do was just wait it out.

There were some soft moaning sounds from above, and I could tell Mrs. Warner was leaning over the railing, trying to spot the ghost of her dead son as he roamed the grounds—a lost, tormented soul walking the earth, haunting his mother.

Finally, the door creaked shut again, and Mackenzie and I were able to make our escape. My leg had recovered by then, and we both ran as fast as we could until we were sitting at one of the Formica tables at the original Bob's Big Boy—a real Toluca Lake landmark, complete with the original sign and a commemorative plaque. We sat there, recovering our wits and our breath, and wolfing down a couple of burgers while we waited for Uncle Dave to show up.

As we ate, we went over what had just happened. "I think she's gone totally ya-ya," was Mackenzie's considered opinion.

"Bonkers," I agreed. "But do you think she being tormented by a guilty conscience? Or is it just the aftermath of the tragedy?"

"There's a third possibility," she pointed out.

"Such as?"

"She could have *always* been crazy, or on the edge of it—only she was able to hide it from the world. Maybe she was always nuts, and that's why she killed Timmy!"

"Well, maybe," I said. "But I bet we'll find out a lot more after we spy on that séance tomorrow night."

"Yeah," Mackenzie said, "something like the fact that Mrs. Warner moonlights as an ax murderer."

8

House of Pancake

Uncle Dave's shoot ran late. By the time he picked us up, we'd had sundaes for dessert, and were practically asleep right there at the table. We'd both forgotten about jet lag—it was three hours later as far as our bodies were concerned.

I, for one, slept like Rip Van Winkle in the car, all the way back to Dave's digs in Santa Monica. I know this because he had to shake me awake when we got there. I sleepwalked to bed, not even noticing his apartment until I woke up the next morning.

It was an open, sunlit place, with a balcony fronting on a quiet block with tall palm trees. But having said that, I have to tell you that Uncle Dave is a really lame housekeeper. He'd bragged in the car about how he'd cleaned up the place—and I guess he'd dusted and swept the floors and all—but I've never seen so much junk piled up anywhere, other than my own room at home. Videocassettes were everywhere, along with sound equipment, cameras, viewfinders, rolls of film, coils of cable, even a couple of awards and trophies for work he'd done in 1991 or something. Add to that every book and magazine Dave had read in the last ten years, at least two months' worth of junk mail . . . I don't think Dave ever threw anything out in his life.

Everything's a treasure to him, I guess—I feel the same way myself sometimes. But if this was how my digs were going to look in twenty years, I knew right then that I'd better reform my ways, or else rent a barn for storage.

Not that it mattered. Mackenzie and I weren't going to be spending much of our time here, except for sleeping. Over breakfast in Dave's sunny, cluttered kitchen, we planned our day of investigation.

I could see that Dave was going to be a big help to us in a lot of ways. For one thing, he had enough cameras and sound equipment to lend us a camcorder and a Polaroid camera for the séance that night, so we could record any incriminating evidence that came up—or any signs of supernatural activity, for that matter.

Another way Dave came up big for us was that he had access all over town—including the studio lots at Sony, Paramount, and Universal. Timmy's sister, Marina, was shooting a small part in a movie that was filming at Universal Studios. (This much we'd gotten from Jesus, who had made a search of Variety Online for us.) Since we had no idea where Marina lived, and since her number was unlisted, this was going to be the best, if not the only way of getting to talk to her.

The problem was, no one was allowed onto the Universal lot without authorization. Which is where Dave's networking came in so very handy, you see. He was able to make a quick call and get our names on the list, courtesy of a producer who owed him a favor.

Lastly, Dave was serving as our chauffeur around town—and believe me, in L.A., if you don't have wheels, you're totally grounded. In fact, on our way to Universal (which is in Burbank, way across town from Santa Monica, and almost back to Toluca Lake, where we'd been the night before), Dave made an excellent suggestion.

"You know what? You guys ought to rent a couple of scooters while you're out here."

"Scooters? You mean, like, motor scooters?" Mackenzie asked.

"Yeah," Dave said, smiling. "I mean, you can't take them on the freeways or anything, but you can get around pretty well through the streets, and you wouldn't be dependent on me for rides as much. . . ."

"Really?" Mackenzie asked.

"Sure," Dave said, "as long as you rent bikes with less than fifty-cc engines, wear helmets, and stay off the freeways."

"Cool!" said Mackenzie. "I've always wanted a scooter, but I've never ridden one before. Have you, P.C.?"

"Once, in the Greek islands," I said. "It was awesome— of course, there wasn't much traffic there, other than a few donkey carts. But hey—life is an adventure, right?"

Besides, it would be more practical than waiting around for Dave to finish his jobs and pick us up. Falling asleep at Bob's Big Boy the night before was not something I wanted to repeat.

We stopped off at a place about half a mile from the studio entrance on Lankershim Boulevard and rented a pair of Tomos Targa mopeds, complete with motorcycle helmets. Mackenzie got a red machine, and I got a black one. Dave then pointed us toward Universal Studios, and took off for his morning shoot.

The reason we were so hot to interview Marina Warner was this: Timmy's surviving family numbered two—and Mrs. Warner wasn't looking too coherent at the moment. So, despite Marina's reputation of being a couple eggs short of a dozen, we had to believe she was our best chance of getting the inside story of Timmy's family, and some idea why Mrs. Warner had come out to the "left coast" to live.

The guard at the Universal gate gave us our guest passes, and directed us to Soundstage #17 that was all the way on the other side of the property near Spielberg's enclave. We passed the permanent movie sets for *Psycho* and *Jaws*. One was a perfect replica of Greenwich Village in New York; another was a Mexican piazza; a third looked like a South Sea island, complete with blue lagoon where they used to film *Gilligan's Island* and *Fantasy Island*.

"This place is surreal!" Mackenzie said, pulling up on her moped.

I think we were the only two people there who weren't in the movie business. A motley crew of actors, screenwriters, gaffers and best boys, directors and producers, wheelers and dealers, all crisscrossed our path as we putt-putted toward the soundstage, where Marina was playing a bit part in a movie called *Beach Babes in Babylon*. From the title, I could tell it was going to be a major contender for the Oscars—NOT.

But hey, Marina was a relative unknown, and I guess she had to be happy with any part she could get. A job, as they say, is a job.

We found her in a tiny trailer outside the soundstage, being fitted for a bathing suit that was, in my humble opinion, way too small for her. She looked fairly convincing as a Beach Babe, even with her pancake face.

"Marina Warner?" Mackenzie asked.

Marina turned her bleached-blond head our way and gave us a quizzical look. "Do I know you?" she asked in a breathy, anxious voice.

"We're from New York," I said. "Friends of Timmy's."

Marina's right hand involuntarily flew to her throat as a look of fear shot through her like electricity. Turning to the wardrobe mistress, she said, "Give me a minute, will you?" Then she led us outside, saying, "Let's go to my trailer, where we can talk in private."

She led us to an even smaller trailer. The inside was divided up into three or four tiny cubicles—bit-player housing. The three of us squeezed into Marina's little stall. She shut the door behind us, then sat down, taking up the room's only chair, which was propped in front of a makeup table, complete with lighted mirror.

"So, you knew Timmy," she said, clasping her hands together and sniffing back tears in a reasonable facsimile of grief. "And you came all the way out here to pay me a condolence call?"

"Um, not exactly," I said. "We're touring the lot with my uncle, and we heard that you were here. We wanted to tell you how really, really bad we feel about what happened."

"Oh, I know—it's devastating!" she breathed, her lips trembling.

"We were there that day," Mackenzie said. "It was so awful. Your mom . . . she was, like, destroyed."

"Omigod, she's a mess!" Marina concurred, nodding slowly. "She's been really torn apart."

"Yeah," I said. "We were wondering if that had anything to do with why she, um, packed all her stuff up in such a hurry and came out here."

"Well, yes," she replied, wiping a tear from her eye. "She wanted to be with me. Not that we were that close or anything—but after all, I'm the only one she's got left."

"It must make you awfully upset to see her like this," Mackenzie said.

"I'm real worried about her," Marina acknowledged. "I've been thinking maybe she needs . . . you know, some serious help. Like maybe going away someplace for a while."

"You mean . . . put her in an institution?" I asked.

Marina shrugged and sighed. "I don't know—what do *you* think?"

Mackenzie and I exchanged glances. "That . . . *might* be a good idea," I said tentatively, not sure where Marina was heading with this.

"Of course, I'd have to get a power of attorney to have her put away," Marina told us. "Which means getting her to a doctor, and . . . having witnesses testify to her mental state." She gave us a hopeful look.

"Hmmm . . ." I grunted noncommittally. "I understand that . . . you've had your own problems in the past." I was being careful, wanting to prod her but not too hard.

Marina looked down at the floor, getting upset for real this time. "I—I spent a week in Creedmore, if you must know," she said, starting to cry. "My mom put me in there . . . to keep me from . . . you know . . . hurting myself."

"Oh . . ." Mackenzie said. And with that, the conversation came to a screeching halt. Neither of us knew what to say, and so we just waited for Marina to elaborate. But she didn't stop crying.

"Was it about . . . I mean, was it that you wanted to be an actor?" I asked.

"No!" Marina said. "Just the opposite! She kept pushing me and pushing me!" The anger exploded out of her so suddenly that we both backed against the wall of the tiny room, which was covered with outfits hung on hooks. "She used to want to be in show business herself, but she never made it. Once she was a dancing pack of Kool cigarettes, that was it. And then Dad left her flat, and she was broke, so she tried to push us kids into acting so we could make money for her!"

Marina burst into sobs again, and covered her face in her hands. "Money, money, money, that's all she ever cared about—never about us! And now Timmy's dead!"

More tears, and more silence from me and Mackenzie.

"I'm sorry . . ." Marina said, sniffing back the tears. "I can't talk about it anymore—it's just . . . too painful. But thank you for coming . . ."

It was the signal for us to go. I glanced at Mackenzie, and I could tell that she wasn't ready to leave it at that. Neither was I.

"Marina," I said gently, "did you know that your mom took out a three-million-dollar insurance policy on Timmy's life?"

"*What?*" Marina gasped, her face a mask of shock. "Insurance policy? I didn't know anything about any insurance policy!"

As Shakespeare said, "The lady doth protest too much, methinks." I had a funny feeling Marina knew more about the insurance policy than she was telling.

"Of course, we're as concerned as you are about your mom's mental health," Mackenzie said. "We've heard she's going to have a séance tonight, to try and contact Timmy from the other side."

Marina glanced up. "Séance?" she asked. Her flat face suddenly went blank, but I could tell she was calculating something. "Really . . . ?"

"She hasn't contacted you about it?" I asked.

"Me? No. Why would she?" Marina asked. "She knows I'm not, like, superstitious or anything. I don't believe in ghosts. Never did, even when I was a kid. *People* are what's scary, in my opinion."

"I've got to agree with you there," I said.

"Well, it was nice meeting you both," Marina said, dismissing us for the second time.

"Thanks for taking the time to talk to us," I said. "And . . . good luck with your career."

"So sorry for your loss," Mackenzie said, leaning over Marina's shoulder and giving her a hug.

As we walked back to where our scooters were parked, I said, "What did you make of her?"

"She's hiding something, for sure," Mackenzie replied.

"You think she'll show up at the séance?"

"Maybe."

"Too bad we don't know where she lives, so we can watch her movements."

"We *do*," Mackenzie said. With a smug smile, she held up her note pad. On it was a scrawled address: 20340½ Driftwood Alley, Venice Beach.

"Where'd you get that?" I asked, amazed.

"I read it off an envelope on her makeup table," Mackenzie said, "when I hugged her good-bye."

"And here I thought you'd found a place in your heart for the poor little starlet. Mackenzie, you are so bad!"

"I am not!" she said, grinning. "You'd have done the same thing, if you'd have thought of it."

I had to admit, she was right.

9

The Undead

Mackenzie and I both figured that our next move ought to be snooping around Marina's place. Not that we were planning to break in or anything—but you never know. Some people are just naturally trusting, and leave their doors unlocked, or their windows slightly ajar. If that's not an open invitation to an amateur detective, I don't know what is.

Anyway, we'd heard all kinds of incredible things about Venice Beach, and there didn't seem to be many other avenues to pursue between now (around noon) and that night's séance at eight. So we decided to take the long ride to the ocean, checking out the sights of L.A. as we went.

Now, if you've never ridden a moped or a scooter, let me say this—it's totally different in a big city from what it is on a barren Greek island. The slipstream from some of the passing cars was enough to blow my little vehicle sideways halfway across the lane. As we motored toward the Hollywood hills, I could hear Mackenzie in front of me, shouting "Whoo-hoo!!" as her hair flew out behind her helmet.

We were in L.A., we were on our own, we had wheels, and life was beautiful. We could have been dead, like poor Timmy, right? And with the traffic along Ventura Boulevard, maybe we soon *would* be.

We made it up into the Hollywood Hills alive, at least. The road narrowed, then rose above the smog and the noise, winding past the cliffside mansions of stars and power brokers—mansions perched on cliffs, overlooking the vast city.

Our mopeds struggled to climb the hills, but going back down, on our way into Hollywood, was a blast—twisting and turning down the winding road, shouting into the wind.

Our route led us down Hollywood Boulevard, where we gawked at Ripley's Believe It or Not Odditorium, and at the stars' footprints in front of Mann's Chinese Theater. I pointed out Steve McQueen's prints, and reminded Mackenzie about his famous motorcycle ride in *The Great Escape*. She was more interested in Mel Gibson's. We stared up at the famous HOLLYWOOD sign on the hills above, where we'd been riding a few minutes earlier, and I remembered reading about a starlet who'd jumped to her death from the top of the letter D.

"Is this not totally awesome?" Mackenzie asked. "Could you *live* here? *I* could."

"Totally," I said. Nothing like being on our own, with our own wheels and a case to solve.

We drove past Fairfax, the most New York-y part of L.A., with its bagel places and flea markets, and onto Sunset Boulevard. From there, it was straight west, by the House of Blues, the Viper Room, where River Phoenix dropped dead, and the former mansion of Jayne Mansfield, who was allegedly decapitated by a Mack truck. We drove all the way to the Pacific Ocean.

By the time we got to the beach, it was almost two o'clock, and we were both starving. We bought some chili dogs, and sat on the Venice Boardwalk, watching the freak show go past—breakdancing Rollerbladers with freakazoid hairdos, skateboarders doing handstands and acrobatics, madmen, walking tattoo exhibits, gawkers, and burnouts. There were dozens of street performers, too—body-painted mimes, fire jugglers, clowns on stilts, storytellers, singers, bands, unicyclists, break-dancers—you name it.

"Man, I can just picture bringing George Washington back from the dead and showing him this—he'd flip his white powdered wig," I said, my eyes following a unicyclist as he spun around and around at dizzying speed. "Hey, I've gotta try that sometime," I added.

"I can just see you now," Mackenzie said with a laugh.

We stood there for a few minutes more, watching the river of people flow by us. Then I remembered why we were there. "Do you really think she killed him?" I asked.

"We both know she did, P.C.—that's why we're here."

"We don't *know* that she murdered him," I pointed out. "That's just the point. He *could* have fallen in on his own."

"She's acting awfully guilty for an innocent woman. And if we want to have a look at Marina's place while she's still at work, we'd better do it soon. I mean, she could get back here a lot quicker than we did on our scooters." Mackenzie downed the ice-cream cone she'd ordered after finishing her chili dog, and followed me down the boardwalk.

Mackenzie has the kind of metabolism that allows her to eat absolutely anything and not gain any weight. She is the only girl I know who isn't constantly thinking about losing that extra five pounds—and believe me, that's one of the most refreshing things about her.

"So let's see . . . where does Marina live?" she asked herself, pulling out her pad and looking at the address. Then she got up and went over to this guy who was smoking weed right there on the boardwalk, and asked him for directions.

The guy, who was obviously not all there, studied the piece of paper, nodding at it as if it contained the secrets of the universe, and finally pointed south and east.

"Thanks!" Mackenzie said. "Okay, P.C., let's get back to business. But I warn you—we're going surfing later."

"*Surfing?*"

"How can you come to California and not go surfing, once you're at the beach?" she asked, her hands on her hips. "Just *look* at those waves out there! Just look at those surfers! Don't they seem like they're having fun?"

I looked. About a dozen people in wet suits were zigging and zagging in front of what looked like medium-size waves. I have to admit, it looked pretty cool. After all, I'm a decent skateboarder, and I've snowboarded several times without killing myself. A board is a board, right?

"You're on," I said. "But don't be upset if I pick it up quicker than you."

"Yeah, like that could ever happen," she said, smirking. "We both know who's a better athlete."

We got on our mopeds and rode inland, down a maze of pedestrian alleys lined by quirky little bungalows, painted in odd combinations of colors, and dressed up with little individual touches, like walls of glass bricks, chartreuse trellises, and hedges cut in the shapes of animals. Eventually, after going in circles a few times, we found Driftwood Alley, and Marina's place—a pink-and-lime green bungalow that was one of three grouped around a tiny fountain.

We parked our mopeds and walked up to the front window. It was locked, as was the door. But we did get a pretty good peek inside, thanks to the sunlight that poured in through the kitchen jalousie windows in back.

Marina Warner lived alone, it seemed—there was only one name on the doorbell. And by the look of things, she didn't have too much to call her own. What little furniture there was looked like it had been carefully selected from castaways people had left on the street for the haulers to pick up. There was a cracked Formica table with mismatched chairs, a frayed futon couch-bed, some plastic milk crates stuffed with books and clothes, and not much else.

Obviously, the small parts she occasionally got in films weren't enough to afford her a luxurious lifestyle. Maybe now, with the money from Timmy's trust fund, she'd be able to move up in the world a little.

One thing I did notice that struck me as important: on the kitchen counter were several plastic vials of prescription pills. "Nervous girl," I muttered to Mackenzie.

"What?" she said, squinting her eyes so she could see inside better.

"I was remarking about all those pill bottles."

"I guess you wouldn't be so mentally healthy either, with a mother like that," she commented.

"Well, we're not going to get much more information here, I don't think," I said, looking up and down the alley. I was starting to feel a little self-conscious about snooping around Marina's house.

The street wasn't exactly deserted. Down the alley, a woman was watering her lawn of cacti and aloe plants. A young woman was walking her miniature dachshund. Two kids were tossing a rubber football back and forth. "I think we should get out of here."

"Totally," Mackenzie agreed. "I saw a surf shop near the ice cream place. Let's go catch us some waves!"

Twenty minutes later, we were stepping into the freezing Pacific, wearing semiwet suits and carrying surfboards under our arms. If you've never carried a surfboard, let me tell you something—they're *heavy*! I was glad when we got out far enough that we could lay them down on the water and start paddling seaward.

We got out past the breakers, and joined a group of about half a dozen surfers. "I guess we should have paid for lessons," Mackenzie said as she watched them surf effortlessly through the curling waves, which looked a whole lot bigger up close than they had from shore.

"We'll figure it out," I assured her, with more confidence than I actually felt. "Let's watch them, and just do what they're doing."

Easier said than done. None of these other surfers were beginners, that much was obvious. I lay there flat on my board, watching as one after another, they got up on their boards and caught waves.

No point in waiting any longer, I figured. Grabbing the sides of the board for balance, I quickly came to my feet as a wave rose beneath me. "Whoooaa!!" I yelled as I flailed my arms, struggling to stay vertical. In seconds, the board went out from under me and shot skyward, while I tumbled off and was swallowed by the water.

When I came back to the surface, my board was twenty

feet away and I realized it could have decapitated me. I swam to it and struggled to get back on. All the while, I could hear Mackenzie laughing from a hundred feet away. "Why don't *you* give it a shot, Gidget?" I yelled.

"Watch me!" she said smugly. She pointed her board toward shore, then caught a wave that was quite a bit bigger than the one that had thrown me. I have to hand it to Mackenzie—she actually managed to zig and zag for about ten seconds before she went head over heels into the deep.

"Not bad!" I said as she came paddling back out to where I and the other surfers floated, waiting for the next wave.

"Thank you, thank you," she said, mock humbly.

Then, suddenly, she looked past me, into the middle distance. "Um, P.C.," she said, staring fixedly now. "Check out that blond hottie over there."

I paddled my board halfway around so I could see what she was looking at. About fifty yards from us, a beefy guy with long, platinum-blond hair and black roots was sitting on his board, waiting for a wave. "Yeah? So?" I asked.

"P.C., who does he look like?"

I squinted into the lowering sun, trying to get a better look at the guy. "He does look kind of familiar."

"Take off about ten pounds of muscle, okay—and get rid of the beard and the long blond tresses. Picture him with short dark hair and clean-shaven. *Now* who does he look like?"

"*Oh. My. God,*" I muttered.

"You see?" Mackenzie paddled up alongside me. "That's *him*," she said. "That's *Timmy Warner.*"

10

Hummer

Mackenzie and I tried waving to the guy, shouting Timmy's name. But surf is loud, and the wind was blowing in the wrong direction. *If* he heard us, he gave no indication.

So we tried maneuvering our boards to get closer to him, but the ocean just kept heaving up more waves— and since we weren't surfers, really, we had no way of turning the surf to our advantage.

"We'd better just ride a wave into shore, and wait for him," I told Mackenzie.

"Good plan," she agreed.

That took a lot longer than we thought, though. We probably would have gotten in more quickly if we'd just paddled. When we finally hauled up on the beach, we dragged our boards up onto the sand and turned to look for Timmy's clone.

But where was he?

"He's gotta be out there somewhere," Mackenzie said, shielding her eyes with her hand. The sun was getting low in the sky now, shining right at us. Not good for surveillance.

There were half a dozen or so boarders out there that could have been him. But from this distance, at least, none of them looked like they had blond hair.

I turned around to face Mackenzie. Behind her, in the parking lot, was our guy, stowing his board in the rear of a brand-new red Hummer.

"There!" I yelled, pointing, and we both took off at full speed.

"Hey, come back here!" yelled the guy who had rented us the wet suits and boards. "Where do you think you're going?"

We just kept running. There was no time to explain. The blond guy who looked like Timmy was getting into the Hummer and revving up the engine. Now he was pulling out of his spot, and heading for the exit.

Mackenzie and I hopped on our mopeds and started them up. I don't know what we were thinking—that we were going to keep up with this dude in Pacific Coast Highway traffic?

But the chase never even got started. The Hummer crossed the road and made a left, heading north. We got to the exit seconds later, but found our way blocked by five straight minutes of speeding southbound traffic. Timmy—or whoever he was—was long gone and out of sight.

"Where do you two think you're going with my wet suits!?" the guy from the rental shack asked, putting a hand on each of our shoulders.

"This guy just left the parking lot who looked just like Elvis!" I explained, saying the first thing that came to mind. "We were trying to get a closer look and see if it was really him."

"Sure, sure," said the guy, unimpressed. "Well, get them off and you can have your deposit back." He walked us back to his shack, muttering under his breath in disgust.

Back in our own clothes, we headed back down to the surf. Some of the other surfers were coming in now, calling it a day as the sun went down. We approached one of them, a tall, skinny guy with long black hair and a beard and a gold hoop earring. "Yo!" I called out to him.

"Yeah?" He was massaging his wet hair with a towel.

"You know that dude who was here before—the one with the blond hair, drives a red Hummer?"

"Who, Humphrey? Kinda. Not really."

Mackenzie jumped in. "How long has he been surfing around?"

"Not long, man," the guy said, pulling a tie-dyed T-shirt over his head and slipping into a pair of Vans. "Couple of months, maybe . . . could be less than that. He just kinda showed up one day, blended into the scene, y'know?"

"Uh-huh," Mackenzie said. "I'm Mackenzie, by the way. And this is P.C."

"Nero," the guy said, shaking her hand, then mine. "P.C., huh? What are you, politically correct?"

I grunted at his lame joke (which I'd heard plenty of

times before, believe me). "He looks like a friend of ours from back east. Wrong name, though."

"If you learn anything more about him, we'd love to talk to you some more," Mackenzie said. "Do you hang around here a lot?"

"Mostly," Nero said. "I'd give you one of my business cards, but they're all wet," he joked, pulling his pocket inside out.

"Thanks, dude," I said, "we've gotta take off. Catch you later."

We unlocked our mopeds and revved the engines before pulling out into traffic.

"Do you really think it was Timmy?" I shouted over the din of the motor.

"If it wasn't, why did he run from us?"

"Well, he didn't exactly run," I pointed out. "Could be he was done surfing and it was time for him to go home."

"True, he never actually broke into a run—or even looked hurried. But the timing of his exit was . . . shall we say, coincidental?"

"They never did find Timmy's body," I mused. "Just the shredded clothes. And then there's the matter of his mom, talking to him on the phone last night. I mean, obviously, *she* must think he's dead, since she called a psychic to order up a séance. But what if she's *wrong*? What if he's still *alive*?"

"P.C.?"

"What?"

Mackenzie pulled up alongside me at a red light, lifted her visor, and looked me in the eye. "I've got chills on the top of my head," she said. "It's him."

While my uncle Dave slaved over the burrito dinner he'd decided to whip up for us, I phoned Clement Hall at Northeast Insurance, to fill him in on our investigation.

"Sure, I remember you!" he said cheerfully in his hearty actor's voice. "How are you two kids doing? Getting over the loss of your friend okay?"

"Um, actually, we're not all that sure he's really dead," I said bluntly.

There was a long silence on the other side of the line. Then, "Come again?"

"We think we may have spotted Timmy, alive and well, out here in Los Angeles," I explained.

"You're in Los Angeles?" came the stunned response. "You didn't . . . you didn't go out there just to track down Mrs. Warner, did you?"

"Not at all," I lied. "But we happened to see someone who looks a lot like Timmy here. We're thinking there's a possibility of insurance fraud."

"I see." Mr. Hall's voice had taken on a hard edge. "Look. I don't want to discourage you kids, but I don't think you ought to be spending your parents' money running all over the country on a wild-goose chase."

"This is no wild-goose chase!" I insisted. "Aren't you

at all interested in knowing whether your company paid out a million-dollar settlement for nothing?"

"Of course I am." Mr. Hall's voice had regained its characteristic smoothness, and it was clear that he was now humoring me. "Well, tell me, then. What's your theory? Is this all a massive insurance fraud by Mrs. Warner? Is she living in some fabulous mansion, hiding her supposedly dead son in the closet?

"Look, son," Mr. Hall said—boy, was it annoying when he called me that. "You'll have to do better than that if you want us to launch an investigation of insurance fraud. I mean, when you first came to me, you were accusing Mrs. Warner of murder, if I recall. Now you say her son is alive. Well, which is it?"

"We're not sure what's going on," I admitted. "But we are sure there's something bizarre about this case. Mrs. Warner is acting very guilty—in fact, she seems to be cracking up. Her daughter is totally on edge—and believe me, Mr. Hall, we saw Timmy—we are not making this up."

Hall sighed audibly. "Look," he said in a heavily patronizing tone, "our company happens to be opening a West Coast branch, so it wouldn't be a total waste of time for me to fly out there. But you'll have to come up with some hard evidence if you expect me to drop what I'm doing and take a look at the Warner case. Otherwise, I'm afraid I'll have to ask you not to call me again." And with that, he hung up on me.

11

Kindred Spirits

"What a guy," I muttered, putting the phone back in its cradle. Then I filled Mackenzie in on the conversation.

"How rude!" she fumed.

"He wants evidence, he'll get evidence," I said.

"And we'll get twenty-five big ones!"

"Burritos!" Dave called from the kitchen. "Who's hungry?"

I have to say, there's nothing like a long day of investigation and frustration to work up an appetite. Mackenzie and I wolfed down Dave's Devastating Burritos until we were stuffed.

Dave sat there grinning—the proud chef. "Now," he said when we were done, "where can I take you guys tonight?"

Dave dropped us off around the corner from Mrs. Warner's place, and went off to visit a friend in Studio City. We arranged to call him on Mac's cell phone when we were ready to be picked up. Then Mackenzie and I approached the apartment complex on foot.

From the street, we could see that Mrs. Warner's drapes were drawn, but the flickering light of many candles filtered through them. "Looks like we're right on time," I commented, motioning for Mackenzie to follow me up the stairs.

I went up to the window with Uncle Dave's camcorder, and zoomed in on the crack between the drapes. Mackenzie positioned herself at the door.

"They're in there, all right," I whispered. "Looks like three of them—Mrs. Warner, Marina, and, I guess, the psychic."

"What are they doing?"

"They're sitting around a table with their hands touching."

"Sounds like a séance, all right." She pressed her ear to the door.

"Can you hear what they're saying?"

She listened for a while. "She's calling to him. Over and over again, begging him to speak to her!"

Through the videocam, I could see that Mrs. Warner had her eyes closed, but tears were streaming down her cheeks anyway. Her mouth was moving, and she was leaning forward, her face tilted upward.

Then, all of a sudden, her eyes flew open, and so did her mouth. I didn't need to have my ear to the door to hear the scream that came out of her. I'm sure all of Toluca Lake heard it.

"It's him!" Mackenzie whispered, breathing hard. "C'mere and listen!"

Abandoning the camera for a moment, I pressed my ear to the metal door, and what I heard sent shivers up my spine.

It was Timmy's voice—echoing through the room. It was weird sounding, but there was no doubt that the voice was Timmy's. "Why, mother?" the voice said. "Why did you do it? Why did you kill me? Why? Why? Why?"

Mrs. Warner screamed again, and again. I ran back to the window in time to see her standing in the center of the room, tearing at her hair, her eyes wild with fear and hysteria. "Get out!" she cried. "Everyone get out of here, now! Leave me alone! I can't take it anymore! Go away, I tell you!"

Marina and the psychic, a tall African American lady with a turban, were already backing toward the door. I grabbed the camcorder and pulled Mackenzie down the walkway. The problem was, there was no place to hide.

There were already one or two doors opening along the walkway, so we couldn't head that way. Down the stairs? Marina and the psychic would probably be using that route. That left only one way out—*up* the stairs. I took the steps two at a time, Mackenzie right behind me.

We got half a flight up, and peered over the concrete balustrade to see what was happening. About a half second later, the apartment door slammed open, and out came the psychic, hustling down the walkway, muttering to herself.

Marina backed out behind her. She was still trying to calm Mrs. Warner, but she was acting pretty freaked out herself. Hearing Timmy's voice couldn't have been too good for her emotional stability. After a few seconds, she turned tail and ran down the stairs. Mrs. Walker stood in the doorway for a long moment, then stepped back into the darkness within.

"What do we do now?" Mackenzie asked. "Which one do we go after?"

The psychic was nowhere in sight. I figured she must have turned the corner at the end of the walkway and taken the far stairs. Looking down, I saw that Marina had crossed the lit-up lawn and was standing at the curb, looking down the street for something.

That was weird, I thought. Why wasn't she going to her car? Was she going to turn around and come back up when her mom had calmed down? If so, then what was she looking for in the darkness?

In a moment, I had my answer. Two glaring headlights came barreling down the tree-lined street. A car pulled over in front of Marina, and she opened the door and got in.

"It's a red Hummer!" Mackenzie gasped.

In fact, it looked exactly like the car our Timmy lookalike had escaped in just hours before at the beach.

"Come on!" I yelled, and we sprinted down the stair-case—just in time to see the Hummer screech off into the night.

"Get the plate number!" Mackenzie yelled.

I hoisted the camera and tried to zoom in on the plates. But let me tell you something—trying to zoom in at 100X on a small moving target ain't easy.

"Did you get the number?" Mackenzie asked urgently.

"The last letters looked like SC. We can ask Jesus to check it out later. But in any case, I think we can be pretty sure now that the guy we saw surfing was Timmy. That Hummer came from the street behind the apartment complex, and I'll bet there would have been enough time for Timmy to talk to his mother 'from beyond' and then make his escape."

"So maybe we should check out the back of Mrs. Warner's apartment," Mackenzie suggested.

"Exactly," I confirmed.

Just at that moment, two shots rang out from the direction of the apartment—and the big plate glass of Mrs. Warner's front window shattered into a million pieces.

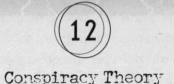

Conspiracy Theory

The door to the apartment was still open. We stepped carefully over the broken glass and up to the entrance, then peered inside, not at all sure it was safe or smart to go any farther.

There were scuffling noises coming from the darkened room. Muffled sobs. Grunts. I could see two people struggling on the floor. One of them had to be Mrs. Warner. The other I recognized through a swirl of psychedelic rayon as the psychic.

I figured they were struggling with the gun. Rather than stand in the doorway like a target, I stepped quickly over to them, reached in, and yanked the pistol out of their hands.

Mrs. Warner screamed in frustration. "Leave me alone! I want to die! Why won't you just let me die?"

"Call 911!" the psychic said in a distinctly Caribbean accent. "She's gone loco! Call 'em, man. Now!"

Mackenzie was right on it, and meanwhile, I helped the medium to subdue Mrs. Warner and pin her to the floor. She was hard to manage, I'll tell you. You wouldn't have thought a woman of her size and weight could punch and kick so fiercely.

"She tryin' to blow her brains out!" the psychic screamed. "If I don't come back in to get me cash, her brains be drippin' down the wall!"

We could hear sirens approaching, weird pulsing ones, like howling coyotes. Soon the paramedics were in the apartment, armed with syringes, asking questions, sedating Mrs. Warner, and getting her all trussed up and onto a gurney for the trip to the nearest psychiatric ward. We answered their questions as best we could, and they told us to wait in the apartment until the police came and we could give them a statement.

The psychic's name was Mama Pearl Cox, and she was from Jamaica. "I know that lady crazy when she call me," Pearl informed us. "I tell her I cannot bring her son back from his watery grave, but she don't listen!"

"Um, Ms. Cox," Mackenzie began.

"Call me Mama Pearl, honey, everybody call me Pearl."

"Mama Pearl," Mackenzie said. "What happened in here during the séance?"

"And who are you?" she asked us, suddenly wondering what we were doing there in the first place.

"We were friends of the dead boy," I told her.

"Did you succeed in reaching Timmy?" Mackenzie asked her.

"Baby, I got the gift," Mama Pearl said, nodding

slowly. "Speakin' with the dead. But this time, things different."

"How do you mean, 'different'?" I asked.

"It were too soon," Mama Pearl said, frowning and shaking her head. "Not like when the dead really talk. It take me by surprise, I tell you. And when the dead speak, it don't echo like that . . . it's more softer, faraway like. This voice were too big—bad juju or bad electronics."

"Mama Pearl, why did you come back?" Mackenzie asked.

"She was so crazy upset, she forget to pay me. And when things go bad, people no want to pay later, you understand? So I turn around and come back—and she got the gun right to her head!" She pointed her finger to her left temple for effect. "She don't need a medium, she needs electroshock therapy or lithium."

The police finally came, acting as if we'd interrupted their coffee break, and we repeated our stories for them—leaving out, of course, our original theory that Timmy was murdered, and our more recent one, that he was alive and surfing at Venice Beach.

Mama Pearl left, after helping herself to a hundred dollars of Mrs. Warner's cash from the top of the bureau—her fee for a séance. She even left a receipt for Mrs. Warner to find, when—and if—she was released from the hospital.

When the police were through with me and

Mackenzie, we went back out onto the walkway that ran down the front of the building's second story. "What do you think?" Mackenzie asked me.

"As I was saying, I think Timmy was here, in the flesh," I said. "And I'm thinking that Marina is in on this thing with him, whatever it is."

"Okay . . . so how did he project his voice?" Mackenzie asked.

"Follow me, Mac." I led her down to the far end of the walkway, where we'd seen Mama Pearl Cox disappear around the corner after Mrs. Warner's episode. The walkway continued down the narrow side of the building—and then around the back. Sure enough, by counting windows, we soon found ourselves outside the back of Mrs. Warner's apartment.

There was no picture window here, just two smaller jalousie ones covered by plaid shades. But there was a vent. Mackenzie bent down to its opening and said, "Helloooo!"

From inside, we heard one of the policemen say, "Whoa! Who's there? Who is that?"

Mackenzie gave me a wink. "Well, I guess we figured that one out," she said. Her eyes scanned the vent and windowsills like lasers. "And hey—lookee here!" She plucked something from the edge of the vent and showed it to me. It was a couple of long, blond hairs.

A perfect match for Humphrey's—or rather, Timmy's!

"Well, Mac," I said, "I think we've just found us some hard evidence of life after make-believe death."

"Jesus? It's me, Mackenzie."

"Yo, where's P.C.?"

"Right here—on the extension." We were using Uncle Dave's phone, so we could both talk to our computer guru at the same time.

"Cool. What's up, you guys?"

"Some really weird stuff is going down out here, Jesus," Mackenzie said. "Like for instance, either Timmy's alive, or a zombie with attention-deficit disorder. He's going under the name Humphrey."

"Huh?"

"Yeah—and he and his sister are gaslighting their mother. You know, deliberately freaking her out," I told him.

"It's like they're giving her the guilt trip of all guilt trips, you know?" Mackenzie said, injecting a little psychological analysis.

"Oh, and by the way, we have a partial license plate for Timmy's Hummer," I said. "We need you to dig up an address where we can find him."

"Sounds good—I'm on it," Jesus said. "Wait—are you *sure* this guy is your friend Timmy? 'Cause you seemed pretty sure he was a total fishburger last time we talked."

"We saw him surfing," Mackenzie told him.

"We chased him, but he got away. We were only on mopeds."

Sometimes I felt a little guilty talking about stuff like this with Jesus. I hoped that someday he would get the chance to drive a really cool vehicle of his own. Although at least now he has a powered wheelchair with all the bells and whistles. But how he got that is another story and another case.

"So what else you got?" Jesus asked us.

"We found a few of Timmy's hairs stuck on the grate behind Mrs. Warner's apartment," Mackenzie said. "Proof that he's been spooking her."

I quickly filled Jesus in on the zany séance. "He cleared out and secretly picked up Marina afterward in his Hummer, and they drove off. That was right before Mrs. Warner tried to shoot herself."

"Are you kidding me? Hey, listen, you guys—take care of yourselves. This case is getting scary."

Mackenzie and I looked at each other. We knew he was right. "We'll be careful, Jesus, but stay in touch," I said into the receiver. "There are a lot of people out here trying to dig graves for each other. Mac and I just have to figure out exactly who wants to bury whom before they starting digging ours."

After we hung up with Jesus, I sat back on Uncle Dave's sofa. "Let's try Mr. Hall again," I suggested. "Maybe now he'll be convinced to fly out here and check things out."

Mackenzie punched in Hall's number. Only after she'd gotten his voice mail did we realize that it was 1:00 A.M. back in New York. Mac left her message anyway, laying out everything that had happened. She finished by telling Hall he'd better get out here if he wanted to save his company a million bucks.

"There," she said as she hung up. "That ought to do it."

I yawned. "If you had any money to gamble, I'd bet you twenty bucks he won't pay any attention."

"I'll have plenty of money pretty soon," she countered, giving me a smug smile. "You're on, P.C."

Jesus called back at five in the morning, our time, with three L.A. addresses whose residents drove red Hummers with SC on their license plates. "Oh, man, sorry I called you so early! I forgot!"

"S'okay, Jesus," I muttered into Mackenzie's cell phone. "I'll wake her up and tell her the good news."

"Do we have to get started this early?" she grumbled, rubbing the sleep from her eyes.

"We've got a few addresses to check out this morning," I reminded her. "And Uncle Dave has an eleven A.M. shoot downtown. After that, we've got our scooters—till late afternoon."

"Aha," Mackenzie said, seeing the light. "Okay, you wake him up."

"Me?"

"He's *your* uncle."

Dave was not pleased. He is, how you say? Not an early riser. But definitely a good sport. He took us back and forth, through all kinds of neighborhoods, tracking down the red Hummers.

The first two we found were dead ends. One belonged to a plastic surgeon. The second was owned by a guy who also owned a junkyard, guarded by a pack of man-eating German shepherds. After this little misadventure, which I leave to your imagination, Uncle Dave had had about enough. He drove us back to his place and dropped us off.

"You kids can take it from here," he said. "The last place on your list is up the coast. Pacific Palisades is north of here, and you can get there pretty easily on your bikes. And I'll be home at four this afternoon, so if you need me after that, I'm around."

We said so long, got on our mopeds, and headed up along the Pacific Coast Highway. Pacific Palisades is a wealthy community tucked in among high hills near the ocean. Our search led us down a quiet, tree-lined street with low ranch houses and fancy cars parked in all the driveways. Parked in front of a nondescript house at the end of the block was a red Hummer.

We parked our scooters and rang the doorbell. To our shock, the door was answered by Marina, who looked like she was going to faint when she saw us. A grumpy male voice inside the house called out, "Who's there?"

Suddenly, there he was in the doorway. No blond hair, no beard, or bulked-up muscles could disguise him at this distance. Our last doubts about Timmy Warner's so-called death were the only thing being laid to rest now.

The Heart of Darkness

The "corpse" stared at us blankly for a brief instant, then his face broke out into a big, wide smile. "Hey, guys!" Timmy said. "I guess you didn't think you'd ever see me again, huh?"

Mackenzie and I stood there, mute and frozen like those painted statues they have on lots of the front lawns around Beverly Hills. Marina had run off inside somewhere, as Timmy said something that amazed us even further.

"Come on in," he said, laughing. "Want some coffee?" He waved us inside. "Don't worry, I can explain everything."

I looked over at Mackenzie as we were ushered into the house. I went first in case Marina might suddenly come charging out of the kitchen with a foot-long butcher's knife or a machete. When she did join us in the living room she was carrying a tray with coffee cups, a pitcher of milk, sugar bowl, and two bottles of Mountain Dew.

It was as if they had been expecting someone.

"You guys look kind of shell-shocked," Timmy said, his laughter scaled down now into barely a chuckle. To me he looked like his mind was calculating at a mile a minute.

"You said something about an explanation?" Mackenzie said.

We lowered our carcasses onto a couch, but kept one eye on the front door.

"We've suspected for a while that you didn't go over the falls," I said.

"As you can see, I didn't," Timmy said.

"What's going on?" Mackenzie demanded to know.

"I've changed my name," Timmy said, sounding as phony as he always did when he was alive the first time. "I've started a new life out here. My name is now Humphrey Meadows. It's going to be my stage name."

"That's not the part we're interested in," I said. "We want to know why you let everyone think you were dead. We had a memorial service for you. All the kids from Westside. A lot of kids had a lot of nightmares about you dying. They had shrinks at the school."

Timmy sat down opposite us in a wicker rocker. "I'm sorry about that part, but everything I've been doing is for my mother."

"She pushed you in, didn't she?" I said. "She tried to kill you for the insurance money. We already figured out that part."

Marina's hands were trembling as she tried to pour

herself a cup of coffee. It was easy for her to see from the expressions on Mackenzie's and my faces that we weren't about to touch anything on that tray of hers.

Timmy didn't answer right away. When he did speak, it seemed it was really difficult for him to find the words. "Mom's already unstable," he said. Marina nodded as she sipped from her cup. Timmy went on. "No matter what she tried to do to me, I know she didn't mean it. There's been a lot of mental illness in our family. My grandmother committed suicide. Most of the Warners have severe depression. I think it's just that we're all artists. But whatever, I had to drop out for her protection. If she knew it was me, that I hadn't died, she might do something terrible to herself."

I decided to let that little nugget sit a few moments. Mackenzie looked ready to sock him.

"Don't you think she'd be happy to know that you're alive?" I decided to lead him on.

Timmy dropped his eyes to the floor as thought he were in a great drama and the camera was coming in for a close-up. "After all the grieving—the guilt of something she did in a heated moment—I was afraid she wouldn't be able to take the shock. I'm afraid it might push her over the edge. As it is, Marina and I are trying to get her committed to an institution where she can get the kind of care she needs." He paused a moment and wiped a tear from the corner of his eye. "Please have some coffee. Marina just made it fresh. Or at least a soda."

"Timmy, how stupid do you think we are?" Mackenzie said.

Timmy looked deeply hurt by that remark. "Why did you say that, Mackenzie? I've always admired you. I've always treated you with respect."

Mackenzie glanced at me. She knows me well enough to read exactly what I'm up to, often before I do.

"How did you live through it, Timmy?" I decided to find out first. "I mean, so many of us saw you go over the falls and head toward the spillway. Those turbines would have cut you to pieces."

"True," Timmy said. "I was incredibly lucky, several times over. First of all, that I didn't hit my head on a rock when I fell into the water. . . ."

"When you were *pushed*," I clarified.

"Right," Timmy said. "I was lucky I didn't die going over the falls. There were rocks below, but I managed to land in a deep pool. I was used to diving twenty and thirty feet on the Westside diving team. I could survive a fifty-foot drop easily if I hit feet first—and I know how to do that in spades. Then, as I was swept around the bend toward the spillway I was able to grab onto a half-sunken tree limb. I hung on for dear life, and I was really in good shape. I clawed and scratched my way back onto the shore."

"What about the shreds of your clothes they found?" Mackenzie asked.

"I threw my jeans and shirt in. The current had been

strong, so I knew enough to slip out of them. I was frightened. I didn't exactly know what I was doing, but I'd done enough camping."

"I remembered you were in the Boy Scouts. You've spent enough time in the woods on camping trips," I said. "You could always handle yourself—so you decided to keep out of sight, double back, and get your backpack and dry clothes."

"Right," Timmy said, looking grateful that I was getting with the program.

"And then you disappeared and came out here," Mackenzie said. I could see she still wanted to reach out and yank him by his ears.

"Where else was he going to go?" Marina cried. She had stopped trembling now that Mackenzie and I seemed to understand. "Who else did he have to turn to after our mother tried to kill him?"

"If she knew I was alive, like I say, I'm afraid of what she'd do to herself," Timmy said.

"Why didn't you just go to the police with this?" I asked. "I mean, if you've got a homicidal mom—you knew she was doing it for the insurance money—then why protect her?"

Timmy sighed heavily. "You guys don't understand," he said. "She's our mom. We love her in spite of everything. We want the best for her, and that means treatment. Rest and therapy. Help, not prison."

Mackenzie shook her head like she wanted to scream.

What Timmy and Marina didn't know was that we'd *been* at the séance the night before. We'd heard Timmy's voice echoing through the room and found his hair on the vent grating in the back. We knew he and Marina were trying to drive their mom nuts. They clearly wanted Mrs. Warner declared loony or, better yet, make her try to swallow the barrel of a gun and blast her head off. With her dead, Marina would inherit all the insurance money and she'd share it with Timmy or he'd flatten the rest of her into a flapjack.

"Just do me one favor, you guys," Timmy practically begged as we got up. "Keep it quiet about me being alive, okay?"

"Come again?" Mackenzie said, thinking she was hearing things. I gave her a stern look to let things ride.

"For our mom's sake, no cops, please," Timmy said with a straight face. "Let Marina and me handle it our way. When we're certain Mom's going to get the care she needs, we'll tell the authorities everything. We promise."

Marina started to tremble again as her head bobbed like some kind of a plastic dunking bird.

"Sure, Timmy," I said. "We can see your point of view." I felt like adding, yeah, man, you want to buy some time until you can get your hands on that money and head over the border for Tijuana or Brazil. "We're just thankful that you're alive."

Timmy locked his eyes on mine. I knew he was

checking to see if I was putting him on or not. Now it was my turn to act, to pretend I didn't think he was one major sick puppy.

"Great," Timmy said. "We can't thank you enough."

"Yes," Marina said, her voice breaking.

"No problem," Mackenzie said through her teeth. She pinched my hand so hard I almost had to cry out.

"Good luck with her—with your mom," I said as I practically dragged Mackenzie out.

"Hey, Mackenzie," Timmy called as we straddled our mopeds and strapped on our helmets.

"What?"

"It's great to see you. Give me a call if you're ever out this way again!"

"Yeah . . . sure thing . . ." Mackenzie replied with a weak little wave. Then she hit the gas and took off down the street.

It took me two blocks to catch up to her. "Nice getaway," I said. "Do you think you could have waited for me?"

"Now what?" Mackenzie asked, ignoring my remark. "I say we go straight to the police."

"Not just yet," I replied. "First I want to call that guy Hall. He's as good as here when we tell him about this."

Mackenzie grinned at me as the light turned green. "P.C., that reward loot is as good as ours!"

Great minds really work in the same direction, because

when we got to Uncle Dave's there was a message from Mr. Hall on the answering machine. "This is for P.C. Hawke and Mackenzie Riggs," Mr. Hall's smooth, deep voice intoned. "I received your urgent message last night. It's now one P.M., and I've just arrived in Los Angeles. Please call me as soon as possible on my cell phone—937-222-2726. I'll wait to hear from you."

Of course I dialed it straight off. Mr. Hall answered, and I starting machine-gunning facts at him. It was a lousy connection, and he didn't want to hear the details on the phone. "Listen," he said, "I'm at the home of the L.A. representative for the company. I want him to hear everything along with me, and we'll all discuss what we're going to do about it and when." Mackenzie shared the phone with me like Siamese phone twins.

"We were just with Timmy," Mackenzie shouted into the mouthpiece. "He's alive all right. And kicking!"

There was silence.

"Mr. Hall?" Mackenzie said, puzzled. "Did you hear what I said?"

"Yes . . ." Hall said. It was like he'd gone into shock.

"Isn't it freaky?" Mackenzie said.

There was a loud clearing of a throat. "Don't say anything more on the phone," Mr. Hall said, finally. "Half of Sunset Strip is spy-equipment shops. Out here they bug everything from phones to the tables at the House of Blues. Can the two of you get out here? We've got the police and FBI notified, but we're going to need to hear what you've got to say. We'll need some kind of a deposition."

"Where are you?" I asked.

"Topanga Canyon," Mr. Hall said. "Just before Carbon Beach. Do you know where that is?"

"Yes," I said. My dad has taken me out there to collect fossils a few times—Old Topanga Road, inland, practically in Tarzana.

"You have wheels?" Hall asked.

"My uncle's not here now or he'd drive us."

Mackenzie hogged the phone a moment. "If we can prove Timmy's alive, there's still a reward for us, right?"

"Yes, of course there would be," Mr. Hall said. I took the phone back, as Hall went on. "I've got to stay with the phones but I could send a car. . . ."

"We've got motor scooters. We could make it out there in about a half hour."

"Good," Mr. Hall said. "We've got a lot of calls coming in here, so I've got to stay with the phones. The address is 1401—the end of Topanga near the Coast Highway. The turn-off is just past the Chart House and there's a Mobil station."

"No problem," I said.

"You know how curvy this canyon is, so drive carefully."

"Will P.C. and I be the only ones splitting the reward?" Mackenzie asked.

Mr. Hall went silent a moment. "Don't worry,

Mackenzie," he said. "You guys will be the only ones getting it."

"Great."

"We'll be waiting for you. Call if you get lost," Hall said and hung up.

"Ya-hoo!" Mackenzie exulted, giving me a high five. "Finally, he got it through his thick skull that we weren't just making things up. Twenty-five thousand, here we come!"

It was now 3:30 P.M. "Dave is due back in half an hour," I said. "Maybe we should wait for him."

"Are you kidding?" she said, her voice rising with excitement. "Timmy and his sister aren't just going to sit around and trust us to keep things quiet."

What could I say? She was right. I left Dave a note, telling him we'd had a breakthrough in the case, and would call him later.

We drove up Pacific Coast Highway toward Malibu Beach, then turned in at Topanga Canyon Drive and headed up into the steep, winding hills.

A warm wind blew into our faces as we climbed slowly upward, the engines of our mopeds struggling against gravity. The sun threw long shadows ahead of us, but the woods and patches of rock and scrub on either side of the road were dark. Hidden in the trees were houses, some grand, some humble. Many of them were perched on the edges of bluffs with a sunset view of the Pacific.

I don't know why, but somehow I couldn't help

remembering that it was in one of those hidden houses—one on Cielo Drive, in another canyon—that Charles Manson and his gang had committed their brutal murders way back in the sixties or seventies, I forget when.

After several hairpin turns, we were quite a ways up the mountain, and too far inland to see the ocean anymore. The sun was setting fast as we came to a mailbox for 1401. We turned onto a dirt driveway that disappeared into the shadows of the trees.

"I've got chills on the top of my head, P.C.," Mackenzie said as we slowed our bikes rounding a bend.

"It feels weird to me, too," I said. "He got out here awfully fast. Isn't that kind of odd, considering that he didn't believe anything we'd said up till now? And if the company has an L.A. rep, why didn't he tell us that before?"

"True. Maybe we should turn around and head back," Mackenzie suggested.

"Nah," I said after a minute's hesitation. "We know we've got something here, and Hall's the guy that needs to take the next step."

We put on our headlights and I followed Mackenzie as we zipped through the woods. There was a quarter mile of open road along a cliff road, then finally, the dirt driveway opened out into a circle in front of a small garage. Beyond the garage was a redwood ranch house facing out over the sheer canyon wall. One side of the sprawling house was a large lighted deck perched on stilts, teetering over the precipice. The house itself looked like it had seen better days, and been unoccupied for some time.

A black Chevy convertible from Southern Cal Rent-a-Car was parked in front of the garage. Leaning against it was Mr. Hall.

"Hi!" Mackenzie shouted as we hopped off our bikes. "You made it! Great!"

"Yes," Mr. Hall said, walking toward us and smiling. "Glad to see you both."

We all shook hands. "So, did you bring your evidence with you?" he asked.

"Here," Mackenzie said, handing him the Ziploc bag with Timmy's hair in it.

"Just this hair, huh?" Hall said, examining it. "I don't know that this by itself would prove anything."

We quickly relayed the whole story of our time in L.A.—including having coffee with Timmy and Marina that morning.

"So . . . you know where they're living? You have an address?"

"Of course." Mackenzie took out her pad and showed it to him.

He tore off the page with the address and stuffed it into his jacket pocket, along with the envelope containing the hair. "Good . . . good," he said, nodding thoughtfully. "I'll be paying a little visit there soon. But first, I want you to meet my L.A. partner."

He led us out onto the deck with its blazing flood-lights, walking straight over to the rail and staring out over the edge, down into the canyon. He motioned for us to join him, and we did, staring at cacti and sage-brush, and the shimmering tops of junipers and cre-osote bushes far below.

"Maybe I'm missing something," Mackenzie said. "What's down there?"

"Nothing yet," Mr. Hall said. "But there will be, soon enough." Turning to the bungalow, he called, "Come on out and join us, darling."

The door of the house opened—and out stepped Meryl Warner!

Mackenzie and I were startled. We turned back to see the glint of a pistol pointed at us.

"You see," said Mr. Hall, "I'm afraid it's *you* who are going to be at the bottom of the canyon."

14

Cliffhanger

Hall was smiling like a demon, appearing highly amused by the stunned expressions on our faces. "Oh, yes," he said. All the facts of the case were falling into place, but it looked like it was really going to be too late for Mackenzie and me.

"Meryl and I have known each other for a very long time, you see," Hall said. He moved to her side, keeping the gun pointed at us.

"Yes," I said. I forced myself to speak loudly and clearly so he wouldn't know I was terrified. As long as I could talk I figured I'd stay alive. "We knew your company had paid off a little too quickly in a case where there was no body."

"Not really," Hall said.

"You had to have helped things along a bit beyond the call of duty," I said.

"Was it love at first sight when Meryl came to your offices to take out an insurance policy?" Mackenzie asked.

Hall looked like he was savoring that question, like it

brought back happy and fond memories. "Meryl and I met when we were just about your age. We were good-looking kids like you two, but not very smart. We weren't allowed to be smart, didn't have your kind of chances. The good news is that we weren't as nosy either. My mistake was going into the insurance business. . . ."

"Not a riveting field, I imagine," I said. "And don't tell me—Meryl's little error was marrying a loser for a husband and eventually finding herself the mother of two ungrateful, egomaniacal kids."

Hall laughed. "You've got a way with a phrase, kid."

Mrs. Warner was staring blankly at the ground, unable to look at Mackenzie or me. I got the impression she was sedated or had a few too many cranberry vodkas at happy hour. I saw Mackenzie's eyes had switched into her high scope mode, looking for someway for us to get out of this mess. All I knew was that I'd better keep talking.

"The life insurance policy was your idea, right?" I asked Hall.

"Bingo," Hall said, smugly. "It was a hard sell at first, but from my first session with Meryl and Timmy I knew it was a possibility. There was no love lost between them."

"No one could pin their hopes on Timmy," I said.

"He wasn't going to share his trust money with her. He treated her like she was his maid right in front of me. His personal whipping girl."

"You started dating her again?" Mackenzie asked. "Like old times?"

Hall put his arm around Meryl like he was hugging a big rag doll. "We met for a few lunches. The Russian Tea Room. We went up to the Cloisters. Sometimes we took a drive."

"He got you to push Timmy into the river to kill him?" Mackenzie shot at Meryl. "What kind of a mother are you?"

Mrs. Warner gave an involuntary shudder, but didn't look up. Mackenzie shook her head in disgust.

"Anyway, you didn't succeed," I said. "Timmy's more alive than ever, and he's not going to let either of you get away with this. He's already done a pretty good job of haunting you, and something tells me he's just warming up."

Hall coughed from the night air. A bright full moon had begun to rise over the north mountain ridge as he smiled again, a hollow, ghastly grin. "We're not worried about Timmy. As soon as we're finished with you, we'll settle our accounts with him and Marina."

Mrs. Warner started whimpering like she had some sort of maternal feelings left, at least for Pancake-face. She started to say something, but Hall cut her off.

"*Won't we*, Meryl?"

Hall spun the gun in his hand. In the glare of the deck lights I could see that it was a small caliber. I knew it could easily kill someone if one of its bullets hit the brain or heart, but it wasn't going to blow a hole in us like a thirty-eight or a forty-five.

"And we told you where they are," I said.

"Yeah," Hall said, chuckling.

"Otherwise you would have had to wait around Marina's bungalow waiting for an opportune moment," I went on. "It's so crowded in Venice. Flimsy walls. Crowds all over. Hard to shoot anyone without somebody noticing. Pacific Palisades is much quieter. You have to kill them both now, don't you?"

"Yep," Hall said.

"Which means they won't be joining you for Tequila Sunrises in Rio, or wherever you plan to disappear to," I said. Hall dropped his hand from Meryl's shoulder and started toward me. "Mrs. Warner, I guess somebody somewhere would notice your kids are disappearing at a bit faster rate than most other parents'. Don't you realize how wacky this whole thing is? Neither of you is going to get away with it. My uncle's heading here right now. I gave him the address. He'll be coming up the drive any second," I said.

Hall laughed. "Nice try," he said. "The two of you actually seem as selfish and self-centered as Meryl's losers. All you two really care about is the reward. I'm sure your uncle's got you two figured out as a couple of free-loaders and big users just like Timmy and Marina."

He raised the pistol up and away from his body, pointing its barrel straight at me. He grasped its handle with both hands, and squinted as he aimed.

You know how your life is supposed to flash before your eyes the instant before you're going to die? Well, I can't tell you every last frantic image that crossed my consciousness at that moment, but I will say that there were definitely not enough of them. The idea of a bullet crashing through my brain made me leap to the right faster than I've ever moved in my life, crashing down onto the deck. There were two other sounds—neither of them a gunshot.

The first was a scream from Mackenzie, which I greatly appreciated. Even as I rolled I could see Hall's head jerk from the sudden, piercing, and painful sound.

And in that instant came the second sound, the roar of Timmy's red Hummer as it broke from the woods and into the straightaway along the edge of the cliff. In the dust and moonlight it looked like a crazy thundering juggernaut out of Mad Max heading straight for the deck.

It was clear that for a split second Hall didn't know what to do, but I did. I threw myself like a wolf at his ankles, locked my arms around them, and yanked with all my strength. I felt like I was tipping a cow, but Hall went down and his gun flew out of his hands—unfortunately straight toward Meryl. But Mackenzie and I didn't need an invitation. We were up and running off the deck as Timmy braked the Hummer hard into a violent skid throwing up a choking cloud of dust. The

Hummer's tanklike front hit the edge of the deck and the whole platform shook like everyone was topside on a tuna boat.

Meryl tried to get the gun back into Hall's hands, but she dropped it. Hall looked stunned now in the high beams of the Hummer. It took him a moment to react. As Mac and I ran through the dirt cloud for our scooters, Hall crawled on the deck to grab the gun again. The doors of the Hummer flew open and Timmy and Marina jumped out. I half-expected them to have swords or sushi knives and try to stick us, but Timmy seemed oblivious to us and made straight for Hall. The insurance guy had recovered his wits by now, and raised his gun at the charging Timmy.

"NOOOO!!!!"

15

The Family That Slays Together

Mrs. Warner's scream echoed off the walls of Topanga Canyon like the cry of a wounded coyote. Mac and I were on our scooters, frantically trying to kick-start them as Timmy was airborne. He landed on Hall like a linebacker on a quarterback. Hall toppled backward, hitting the ground with a thud. The pistol fired, a bullet heading skyward. Timmy twisted Hall's wrist until he dropped the gun, and Marina scooped it up.

"Timmy, just listen to me," Hall grunted, as they rolled over and over each other. They were off the deck now, close to the edge of the cliff. "There's enough money for all of us!"

Mackenzie and I managed to start our scooters and were panicking on top of them trying to shift. I was afraid of Marina now that she had a weapon and might come charging after us like an armed pancake.

"You tried to kill me!" Timmy roared at Hall and his mother. "Both of you!"

Hall saw his opportunity, and crashed his fist into

Timmy's jaw. Timmy cried out, let go of him, and clutched his face howling in pain. The last thing I saw was Hall springing at Marina, grabbing for the gun. Timmy was right after him.

Dust flew as Mac and I hit into gear and gave the scooters full gas. We sped away from the house into the straightaway along the cliff. Seconds later we heard gunshots—two of them!—then three more. We raced away as fast as we could, but moments later we heard a car start and were soon caught in the glare from a pair of high beams. I hoped we could reach the woods, that somehow we'd be able to get out scooters onto a path or fire trail where no car could follow us.

"Faster!" I screamed at Mackenzie in front of me. "Faster!"

"This isn't an airplane!" Mac yelled without turning around.

The car was bearing down on us. "We've got to do something!" I cried.

"Yes!" Mackenzie screamed. "Die—NOT!"

The car kept gaining on us, even though we were going downhill. Two or three times, going around hairpin turns, I thought I was going to go into a skid, and either hit the cliffside, or go over the edge into the canyon. Somehow, Mackenzie and I stayed upright.

It wasn't the Hummer behind us; I could tell by the sound of its engine. This was a regular car. I figured it was Hall's rental car. That was bad news. At least if it had been Timmy, he might not have been trying to kill us. I say *might not*. At this point, I wasn't sure at all where Timmy and Marina stood.

On the other hand, I was totally sure of Hall's intentions. He wanted us dead—which would account for the way he was now driving his car.

"Mackenzie! He's going to try and run us off the road!" I yelled as I took the lead.

"Aaahhhhh!" she screamed.

Right before we hit a blind turn up ahead, I signaled for her to steer hard left. We skidded to a stop in the bushes next to the cliffside. Mackenzie slid in right beside me.

Holding our breath, we both watched as the car tried to react. Hall's first instinct was to zig left after us. Then he began to pull back right—where the road curved sharply.

The rental car went right through a pathetic excuse for a guardrail, and plunged down into the dark canyon below. Moments later there came an explosion. It echoed like thunder, ricocheting off the sandstone hillsides. The light of the flames lit up the sky, making it look like daytime for a split second and we knew that Hall was dead.

Mackenzie was sobbing and rubbing her elbow like she'd banged it pretty good in the skid.

"You break anything?" I asked.

"No," she said. "I'm okay. You all right?"

I tried feeling my arms and legs. "I think so."

"Now what do we do?" she asked, standing in the middle of the road and staring back at the ranch house. Its lighted porch looked like a weird chandelier perched at the edge of the cliff.

I was too dazed to answer, but I gathered my wits pretty quickly when I saw the red Hummer back away from the porch, turn around, and head toward us. Its headlights closed on us like high beams on a pair of bushed raccoons.

"I guess if Timmy wants us dead," I muttered, "this is his big chance."

But the Hummer didn't run us down. It pulled up next to us, and Timmy got out. He shielded his eyes and peered down over the side of the cliff at the burning wreck. Then he turned to us. "You guys all right?" he asked.

"Oh, yeah," Mackenzie said. "Peachy."

"We're fine," I said.

"Good. My sister's back there with Mom. I told Marina to call the police," he said, shaking his head. "This thing has gone far enough."

"I couldn't agree more," I said. "Actually, it's a good thing you followed us here—that was it, right?"

For a moment Timmy looked really sorry about everything that happened. Even Mackenzie looked like she believed he was genuinely repentant about all the mess he'd gotten everyone into. Then he said, "Yes, we followed you. You looked too suspicious and flaky, and we thought you might go tell our mom what we were up to."

"Well, we *did*," Mackenzie shot at him.

"We called Hall's office and clued him in," I said. "We didn't know he was an insurance man psycho at that time."

"Oh," Timmy said, staring back down at the flaming wreck. "Well, all's well that ends well."

"Have you got a screw loose?" Mackenzie brayed at him, furious at his insensitivity. "Don't you realize that Mr. Hall has been turned into a burnt shish kebab? Don't you have any sense of your guilt in this whole insane mess? If you had gone to the police in the beginning and said, hey, guys, I really didn't croak going over the falls—nobody would have died."

"Well," Timmy said, "I'm alive. My sister and my mom are alive. You guys are okay. Four out of five isn't bad."

"Your mother's not alive," Mackenzie said. "You've turned her into a mental zombie."

"We're going to get her some help," Timmy said, "just like I said we would this morning. I don't know what Hall had her doped up with, but my mom hasn't been herself since she met him."

"Timmy," I said, "cut the act. You tried to get your mother to kill herself. We were there outside the séance. We *saw* you. Heard you warbling through the air-conditioner vents. How do you live with yourself, being such a phoney?"

"Yeah," Mackenzie said. "There are laws against mothers knocking off their weirdo kids, but there are laws against matricide, too!"

Timmy's face hardened. "You can't prove a thing."

"You're wrong about that," I said, as we heard the sound of a car coming up from the coastal highway. The lights began to break through the woods and onto the cliff road. "That's my Uncle Dave's car, so, Timmy, what the police will soon have is what we in the detective world refer to as living proof—*you*."

That's a Wrap!

I guess the moment Mr. Hall's car exploded at the bottom of the canyon a few hundred people who lived in the Topanga cliff houses must have run to their phones and called the police. Between that and Uncle Dave calling on his cell phone, our whole end of the canyon was ablaze with cop cars, their roof lights flashing like the strobes of a freakazoid dance club. It boiled down to Police Chief Kyle Storm, head of the Malibu police district, grilling me and Mackenzie while the Warners were each taken away in separate patrol cars. Chief Storm looked a little familiar, and he didn't take long to confide in us that he was a former child star who had done guest appearances on *The Brady Bunch* before going into the law enforcement field.

As it turned out, Mac and I had to stay in L.A. a couple of days longer than we'd planned. Mac and I got her mom to call Westside and explain that we were being detained to give depositions in Los Angeles in an attempted murder and fatality case. We knew how fast that little news item would spread through the school and wreak fresh havoc on our pubescent social life. What took so long was that the Case of the Surfing Corpse was not a matter of whodunit. The cops said it looked like a case of whodidn'tdoit.

"You kids did a fine job," the agent sent out from Northeast Insurance told us. It was Ray Ferraro, the same guy who'd first told us about the reward. Ray was on the L.A. scene in less than twenty-four hours with a couple of other guys in his entourage who looked like they were anoretic accountants. Uncle Dave was with us. He hadn't let us out of his sight our whole rest of the time in Los Angeles. He took a seat off to the side and looked a little stunned.

"Thanks," Mackenzie told Ferraro, but I knew what she was really curious about at this point.

We went over the facts with the insurance guys. It was like everyone everywhere was recording whatever we said. The cops had a tape recorder going. The insurance guys. And when Police Chief Storm had asked the questions they sounded like he was secretly doing research for a future movie-of-the-week docudrama that would star someone like Bette Midler as Meryl Warner.

The deposition we gave Ferraro took place in an office in one of the new Santa Monica high-rises. When we first went in he motioned us toward a couple of spacy leather-and-chrome chairs. Someone came in with a trayful of designer water bottles, plastic containers of carrot juice, and a six-pack of Diet Pepsi. Drinks were served all around. Ferraro settled himself behind a desk that looked like a console from *Battlestar Galactica*. "I've been monitoring Mr. Hall's files for quite some time now," he said, leaning forward. "But I could never find a smoking gun."

"Well, now we helped you find a smoking rent-a-car and a smoking Mr. Hall."

I coughed and looked Ferraro straight in the eye. "So do you think Northeast will get their whole three mil back?"

"Most of it," he said. "Hall and Mrs. Warner had spent a few thousand on clothes, apartment rentals, and plane tickets to Buenos Aires. If they had made it to Argentina, they would have been set for life."

"Is it really that easy to cheat an insurance company?" I asked.

"No," Ferraro said. "In fact, it's very difficult."

"Except when the agent's dating the beneficiary," Mackenzie said.

"Apparently." Ferraro broke into a broad smile, and drew two envelopes out of his pocket. "And these are for you along with the gratitude of our company."

Mackenzie's hands were shaking as she opened her envelope. I guess when we both saw our checks for twelve thousand five hundred bucks each we nearly passed out.

"Thank you," I said.

Mackenzie couldn't speak.

"We've also gotten permission from your uncle to bump you up to first class for the plane ride home," Ferraro said. "I hope you don't mind."

We turned to look at Uncle Dave. He was smiling now, too.

The next morning we were on American Airlines flight number 34 roaring up through a dense fog and into the bright sunshine at thirty-five thousand feet. I know that on some level we were both still shaken from having come so close to buying the farm at Topanga Canyon.

"This is so cool," Mackenzie said, as we lifted our own private little TV screens out from the armrest of our primo seats. I mean, we were sitting right at the front in the area where stars like Matt Damon, DMX, and Uma Thurman usually hang out. Mackenzie pointed out that practically everyone around us was wearing very expensive, extra-supple leather jackets and Ralph Lauren sunglasses. We were stretched out in jeans. Mackenzie was wearing a Day-Glo blouse she'd bought in Venice and I was wearing a sweat shirt that said I'M RUNNING OUT OF PLACES TO HIDE THE BODIES, which I thought was humorous at the time I bought it.

I suppose the main difference we noticed about flying first class was that we were served hot macadamia nuts, a shrimp diablo appetizer, filet mignon, asparagus, caramel sundaes, and a snack of freshly baked chocolate chip cookies with milk, as well as a choice of twenty movie videos. Tourist class got a Meg Ryan movie and an entree that looked like a small burned rodent.

"You know," Mackenzie said, switching videos, "they found out Hall had some sort of a family that lived on Staten Island and didn't even know what he was up to. Wouldn't it be just horrible if he was right beneath us now in baggage on the same plane being shipped back to them in an urn?"

As we were relaxing and enjoying the first part of our reward, I wondered where Timmy, Marina, and Meryl were just then. Police Chief Kyle shaped up to be very informative on that front before we left.

"If the Warners get themselves a team of lawyers like O.J. did, at least Timmy and Marina won't be doing any time in jail for anything. They're already talking about a probation deal for them, you know, the abused kids route. One of the stipulations of their parole would be that they'd have to live with an apparently sane and strict aunt and uncle they have in upstate New York. They'd have to live with them in Albany, which, I understand, is a cruel and unusual punishment of its own."

"What do you think will happen to Meryl?" Mackenzie had asked.

"She's going to have to do jail time at some women's house of detention or something," Kyle said.

"Like a female Sing Sing?" I said.

"Right," Kyle said.

"Hey," Mackenzie said, "it'll be convenient for

Timmy and Marina to visit her, I mean with all of them up the Hudson River like that."

"They have to lock her up to send the right message to all parents: Don't try to knock off your kids for profit." Kyle said. "There's an increasing trend in our society for parents to do that, and vice versa. That's one message that has to get out to all kids. Tell someone if you think your mom or pop wants to whack you."

"I'm sure the Warners will all get some kind of therapy," Mackenzie had said. "Like, I wouldn't be surprised if Mrs. Warner has a whole history of some mental sickness like Munchausen syndrome by proxy—you know, where some mothers make their kids sick so they themselves can become the center of attention when an ambulance arrives but they've already saved them. Something eerie like that."

A couple of hours into the flight the excitement of first class sort of wore off, and I think Mackenzie and I both began to think how lucky we were to have families that loved us and weren't trying to assassinate us. We both took out our checks and gazed at them again. They were so beautiful.

"You know what I'm going to do with my loot?" Mackenzie said. "I'm going to give it to my folks to get that new roof. I mean, maybe I'll spend a couple of hundred in Wearable Art for a faux-jaguar skirt or the Gottahavit recycle shop for a zircon lizard broach. Just a little something for me."

"Cool," I said. I was really touched by Mac's idea. "I didn't know you had that kind of generosity in you." I pressed the light for the flight attendant. I felt like some more roasted macadamias.

"Well, I do!" She smiled slyly. "Besides, this way if our class decides to hold the junior prom in Barbados or Puerto Rico this year, my parents won't have an excuse to say no."

I should have known there was an ulterior motive. You can't change a leopard's spots. You can lead a horse to water, but you can't make her drink. You cannot teach an old dog new tricks. Ah, yes, the old clichés. I told you there was always some truth to them. Especially the one that goes, "There's more to this than meets the eye."